1152

L. S.
Rw

1/17   224

9/17-6267

14/17-1394
RB 10/19- 1394 RT
JR.
D.C.

NIGHT
OF THE
RUSTLER'S
MOON

Center Point
Large Print

Also by Lauran Paine and available from
Center Point Large Print:

The Plains of Laramie
Man from Durango
Prairie Empire
Sheriff of Hangtown
Gunman's Moon
Wyoming Trails
Kansas Kid

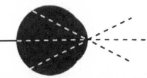

NIGHT
OF THE
RUSTLER'S
MOON

A Western Story

Lauran Paine

CENTER POINT LARGE PRINT
THORNDIKE, MAINE

This Circle Ⓥ Western is published by
Center Point Large Print in 2015 in co-operation with
Golden West Literary Agency.

First Edition
December, 2015

The text of this Large Print edition is unabridged.
Printed in the United States of America
on permanent paper.
Set in 16-point Times New Roman type.

ISBN: 978-1-62899-805-4 (hardcover)
ISBN: 978-1-62899-810-8 (paperback)

Library of Congress Cataloging-in-Publication Data

Paine, Lauran.
  Night of the rustler's moon : a western story / Lauran Paine. —
    First edition.
    pages cm
    ISBN 978-1-62899-805-4 (hardcover : alk. paper)
    1. Large type books. I. Title.
    PS3566.A34N474 2015
    813′.54—dc23
                                        2015033494

NIGHT
OF THE
RUSTLER'S
MOON

Chapter One

They sat up there with the great yellow moon behind them, with one of Wyoming's little freshet winds blowing low along the ground, silent and watchful, the four of them.

Below, burnished by that ancient overhead disc, lay a world of silence, of grasslands running on to a far-off merging with purple-curving heavens. A land of gentle lifts and rises, of trees and tree shadows, a land unchanged since time out of mind. A land of horsemen where simple ethics and simple laws prevailed.

Which was why old Amos McCarthy and his three riders were sitting atop that northward rim, screened from view by wind-twisted old trees, because the simple laws prevailed and over old Amos's right shoulder that huge yellow old moon was as good to see by as it was to hide by. It was a rustler's moon.

Amos was raw-boned and resolute; when that had been said, there was no need to say more. It was in his eyes, in the iron droop of his lipless mouth, in the way he sat his horse atop the rimrocks like some avenging old patriarch of Biblical times with his shaggy mane and his longhorn mustache.

On the right of old Amos, Vern Howten had the

sheep-pelted collar of his riding coat turned up against night cold. Vern was a man in his middle years, dark-eyed with an habitual squint, a good man with a horse, a rope . . . or a gun. He was Amos's range boss. Vern was a good stockman. He was a quiet one, though, and at marking time the others were conscious how he skirted around their jokes and their gibes. He was a man who had, somewhere along the line, forgotten how to smile. It was said in some quarters that was why old Amos had kept him on as foreman of Rafter M—because neither of them ever laughed, ever smiled, ever talked, for that matter, unless they had something which had to be said.

Mick Gleason, directly behind Vern, like Everett Tarr beside him, was in his twenties. Mick was a typical cowboy, rugged, lank, leaned-down from work, with a little quirk to his lips as though he was always on the edge of laughing. He and Everett had been with Rafter M six months; they had come over the Bitteroots together, had hired out together, and sometimes when folks didn't know any better they said Everett and Mick were brothers. They might as well have been, for as Hugh Barnum—the Rafter M cowboy who was not up there with Amos this night—always said, when Mick made a smoke, Everett lit a match; they were that close.

"They're coming," said shock-headed Everett, his head cocked, his eyes swerving toward a

8

shoulder of land that swung westward toward a pure flare of open country. "I hear 'em."

Neither Amos nor Vern beside him acknowledged this at all, but Mick did. He said softly: "Yeah." That was all though, for movement appeared now. A band of free-running horses came plunging around that shoulder of westerly land, a big band with dust spiraling above them to reflect yellow moonlight as spun gold might have done.

Those four men sat there watching that rush of loose stock, their faces grimly set. Each of them was armed with a belt gun, and a Winchester under the *rosadero* in its scuffed saddle boot.

Far southward stood a humped-up mountain range. Where the highest peak of this chain was, a year-around snow field lay above six thousand feet. There, moonlight shone off dirty white, making a ghostly hue, but lower down, the stair-stepped tiers of red-barked pines shown, dark as soot and stiff.

Closer, backgrounded by that far-away rocky upland country, the free-running horses began to fan out, to spread across the grasslands, to slow, eventually, coming down from their hard run to a gradual lessening of their earlier momentum, and after a while to stop, here and there, in groups to graze.

It was a wild, good sight, all those free animals upon that unblemished plain with an ancient coppery moon glowing. It put a man in mind of how the world must have once been, before the white men came.

But beauty is different things to different men. Amos McCarthy looked on that remuda as the fruit of his labor. He owned those horses and he owned that deep-sod plain they were grazing upon. He had spent his life in the service of the land, and he was like Wyoming's uplands—he was craggy and untamed; he was unrelenting and harsh. If Nature in the raw was seldom mild, the same could be said of the men like old Amos that Nature had formed and sustained.

He sat there beside Vern Howten in his old blanket coat as an Indian might have sat, watching, waiting, unmindful of the passage of time, unmindful of the creeping chill as this night wore along toward the small hours, thinking of only one thing in his harsh and narrow way— thinking of that rustler's moon and what it had done to him the previous month when out of nowhere a band of renegades had come swirling down out of the timber, swept across this same range, taking with them thirty of his best horses.

The moon made its impersonal left-to-right crossing, the imperceptible, slow shift of ground shadows went unnoticed, the chill became sharper, all without making any impression upon old Amos or Vern Howten. But behind them Mick and Everett blew on their hands, looked across at one another, shrugged, and sat on until the faint clatter of a shod horse approaching captured their interest and held it. But neither of them said anything. They simply craned around from time to time as that scrabbling sound came closer. They eventually made out the rider where he passed out of trees onto the wind-scourged rim where the four of them sat.

This newcomer was Hugh Barnum, the Rafter M man who had been detailed to chouse that band of loose stock to the east range. Hugh was a slight man in his middle thirties; he had yellow hair, pink skin, and very pale eyes. He had been a Rafter M cowboy for three years. It was said of Hugh Barnum that he had no equal at reining horses in all Wyoming.

He came up beside Mick Gleason, halted and waited, his glance shifting from the back of old Amos to the back of Vern Howten. After three years a man knew what was expected of him and he did it. He would have sat like that until dawn without opening his mouth, if Amos or Vern hadn't spoken first. That's what a man learned after three years on Rafter M.

Howten said quietly: "See anything, Hugh?"

"No."

"You reckon anything saw you?"

"I doubt it. I stayed right in among 'em. They'd have had to be real close to see that there was a mounted man pushing them horses."

11

That was all.

More time passed. Mick Gleason, turning bored, considered that far-away snow field. The coppery tint had altered to a sort of diluted steely blue now. He thought dawn must not be far off. He also thought, dropping his eyes to the plain lower down, that rustler's moon or no rustler's moon, no one was going to hit that herd tonight.

A long distance away a timber wolf stopped on stiffened legs, raised his blunt snout, and let off a lonely howl at the descending moon. Evidently none of his kinsmen was within hearing because he got no reply. An owl came skimming low, seeking rodents. He was following the contours of those same rimrocks where the horsemen sat and did not see them until the very last moment. He emitted a sharp squeak, frantically beat air with his wings, and barely cleared the top of Everett Tarr's hat. Everett ducked, Mick grinned, thankful for even this little diversion, and Hugh Barnum said soberly: "Them cussed things got lice. Once one of 'em hit me like that and I was two weeks washing my hair in sheep dip to get rid of the lice and nits."

Mick's grin lingered. "You must've smelled real fine," he said, referring to the startling aseptic odor of sheep dip. But this went over Hugh's head as much of the customary cow-camp humor did.

"Better to smell like a dipping vat," he muttered, "than be et up by lice."

Everett, impressed by what Hugh had said, removed his hat, held it very close, and peered at it. He muttered some blistering comments about "dumb damned blind owls" and crushed the hat back onto his head.

Throughout all this neither old Amos nor Vern Howten looked back, or even acted as though they knew anything at all had happened. This attitude had its dampening effect on the three rearward riders; they resumed their vigil as before, sitting their saddles like carved statues.

Down below a stallion trumpeted. Every eye hunted for that horse. The stallion whipped upright; he pawed, tossed his head, and trotted out a ways from the nearest animal, halted out there with his tail out, his head up, his whole stance a picture of total concentration.

"Scents something," said old Amos, the only indication that this meant anything to him in the way his fingers tightened on the reins.

The stallion flung his head up and down, whirled, trotted forward a hundred yards, halted, and stood motionlessly, looking on around that shoulder of land westerly. After a moment of this, the horse jerked his head, making his mane whip and toss. He turned, trotted around among the other, disinterested animals, then loped southward until he was entirely apart from the other horses, and took another stand, this time obviously poised for instant flight.

"Sees it now," growled old Amos. "Whatever it is."

Vern Howten finally spoke: "It's horses. Listen."

They all turned quietly attentive for a moment. The next man to speak was Hugh Barnum. He said: "I brought 'em all . . . weren't no more loose ones behind me."

"You sure of that?" demanded old Amos.

"Yes, sir, plumb sure."

"We'll know in a few minutes now. Never was a loose horse sounded like a ridden horse."

That big stud horse down below suddenly wheeled and went in a hastening circle out and around the remuda, seeking to bring them all together so he could drive them away from whatever had troubled him.

"That," pronounced Hugh Barnum, the best horseman in Wyoming, "is good enough for me. It ain't loose stock, Mister Amos. He smells men."

Old McCarthy made no comment to this; he simply looked over at Vern, nodded, and reined his horse around, leading out easterly along the rimrocks toward the downward trail from those overhead heights.

Vern Howten followed in McCarthy's wake and the others trailed after Vern. Off in the saw-toothed east a steely, diluted darkness shown inches above the granite horizon. Mick Gleason, rocking along, thought it must be about 4:30 in the morning. It was colder now, too, even though that little ground-swell wind was no longer blowing.

The entire world was still as death and gloomily softly lit. This was the in-between time—too early for daytime life to be stirring, too late for night life to be abroad.

They came down across a shale rock trail, swung southward on it, and went along until the last lift petered out up the plain. It was dark down here, with a startling aseptic odor from the mouthed cañons. A kind of clammy mist hung above the earth here, too, making it appear that they were riding on top of this milky stuff.

The old man halted when, coming on in a loose run, that Rafter M remuda sent along its preceding drum-roll thunder of many hoofs. For a while they all listened carefully to this unmistakable sound, then Barnum spoke up again, his words reflecting full knowledge of this thing he spoke about.

"They're being driven, Mister Amos. Don't no band of mixed horses ever run full tilt like that . . . every last one of 'em. There's some gutty, bred mares in that band. They'd never keep it up like they're doing now, 'less they were being forced to it."

Amos nodded his shaggy, white head in agreement, but he said nothing. He just sat there, listening until those speeding animals were plainly drawing near.

"All right, Vern, you and Hugh bust across the

front. Break 'em up, then run down the sides. Mick, Everett . . . the three of us'll drive straight along the mountainside here, where they won't be able to pick us out against the background, and we'll cut southerly when we get to the rear of their drive."

Every man's hand tightened a little on the reins. Amos stood in his stirrups, looking westward. He eased back down, loosened the gun in his hip holster, and said: "No quarter. I don't give a damn who they are or what they do . . . no quarter."

Amos swung to look at his bunched-up riders. "All right Vern . . . you and Hugh head out."

Those two eased around their companions, came together ahead of the old man, and kept on, riding slowly at first, then a little faster. Finally they broke over into a lope and were lost in the onward gloom.

Chapter Two

Mick and Everett rocketed along behind old Amos, tense with excitement, both rummaging the southerly night for mounted riders swinging in the wake of that flashing band of running horses.

A gunshot erupted behind them easterly, then another gunshot, this last one a little more to the southward. That would be Vern and Hugh breaking up the remuda by riding head-on into it and firing. There was one more gunshot, then the sound of horses breaking stride, some hauling back, some swinging wide away from those crimson muzzle blasts, still others whipping north or south.

It was a confusing time; no longer was it possible to see all those horses out upon the pale plain. Dust scent filled the predawn air with its pungent rankness. Horses squealed and trumpeted. A big black animal suddenly shot out ahead and raced away in a belly-down run.

Amos left the backgrounding protection, swinging southward. Night light shone off his fisted six-gun. His blanket coat whipped and flopped as he sped along, giving him the appearance of an avenging angel. Mick and Everett, too, reined clear of the mountainside, riding along fast, behind and a little on either side of old Amos.

Somewhere far back and far southward a Winchester laid its sharp snarl into the grayness; two six-guns followed this up with their throatier, booming voices, then, all at once, four guns went off almost simultaneously. Vern and Hugh had encountered the rustlers.

A horse screamed mortally, struck hard by a wild shot. Amos lost his hat and paid no heed. He had someone in view and dug in the spurs to close this short distance. Mick Gleason involuntarily flinched when a gun flamed orange at him off in the saffron east. He threw a shot in that direction.

Amos let off a violent bawl and rapidly shortened the distance between himself and a man atop a big brown horse dead ahead. That stranger whirled from the waist, threw up his gun—and took Everett Tarr's slug high in the body. The stranger lost his gun. He fought hard for balance as his horse shied violently. He made a pass at the tossing mane, missed, and fell heavily to the ground. Old Amos lifted his horse to jump that rolling body. Then he did as the *Ozuye we tawatas*—the Men of War of the Dakota nation used to do—he turned in the saddle as his horse rose up to clear that fallen man, took sure aim, and fired downward. The stranger whipped up rigidly, back arched, corded fingers tearing at the ground, and collapsed inward, turning all loose and flat as Amos raced away.

Mick Gleason swerved around that face-up body. Everett, too, yanked clear. They had only a flashing look at that upward face with its bulging, astonished dead eyes, then the predawn closed around them, bore them farther along in the wake of Amos McCarthy, compelling their attention onward where gun flashes tongued red, tongued orange, in the steely light.

Surprise was an advantage no fighting horseman ever overlooked. Amos McCarthy had chilled the hearts of mighty Dakota fighting men with his fury and his courage in years past. He had always been a believer in surprise and in ferocity. It did not matter to him that the enemy was red or white, simple marauder emblazoned with the bloody Custer on a coup trail, or organized horse thieves, crafty and swift. In the dead of the night, he met them all with the identical tactics as he had done here—with surprise and ferocity, asking no quarter and giving none.

He reined toward two flashing guns, stationary and low upon the plain, and never slackened speed as he approached those frantically firing, unhorsed men. He held his fire, too, long after Mick and Everett, off on either side of him, opened up. Old Amos didn't fire until he saw those unhorsed rustlers, but when he finally did, he emptied his pistol. His gun, in fact, was the last one to cease firing.

Both those rustlers were flat down and finished when Amos slammed his animal down into a long, sliding stop, sat up there atop that quivering beast, glaring downward. Mick and Everett came in more slowly and cautiously. A man could never tell in the night when a downed man was only hurt and possibly playing 'possum.

Amos reloaded as he sat there, letting his empty casings fall in a cascade around the men he'd shot to death. When he finished, he looked around, hefted his handgun, studied his pair of cowboys a second, then said: "Ain't no more firing. It must be all over. Either of you hurt?"

"No," said Mick, stiffly getting down to step across and toe the two dead horse thieves over onto their backs so that the pale dawn light shone upon them.

"Recognize them?" asked Amos, squinting downward.

"No, never saw 'em before in my life," replied Mick. "Ev, come have yourself a look."

Tarr walked up, leading his horse. He looked, then looked away. Neither of those rustlers had died easy; each of their faces was contorted with fear and defiance and something else less simple to define, which might have been purest astonishment that this was unmistakably the end, out here on this god-forsaken prairie miles from anywhere.

"Strangers to me, too," stated Everett.

Hugh Barnum came riding up alone. He studied those two still, grimacing dead faces, shrugged, and put them out of his mind. "Counting them two," he reported to old Amos, "there must've been five of 'em. There's another dead one back northward a ways and I got one, riding up near the front, when we busted the remuda."

Amos listened to this with his eyes probing the round-about night. "Where's Vern?" he ultimately asked.

No one knew, but Hugh Barnum, thinking as he usually thought, said: "The remuda's all right except for one shot horse, Mister Amos. They're strung out all over hell's half acre but we can have 'em bunched quick enough."

"The horses can wait," snapped McCarthy. "They ain't going nowhere. Fan out and let's find Vern. He may be afoot around here somewhere."

The four of them lined out like skirmishers, in a long, straight line from north to south. They rode along at a walk, swinging their heads from side to side. Where loose horses were encountered, these animals, having just survived a terrifying experience, bolted at sight of riders. Otherwise, the night was empty and silent.

Amos raised his arm, halting the line. He threw back his shaggy head and roared out Vern's name. Echoes from that bull-bass thunder ran on and on and on. They sat there waiting for a long time, then an answer came back muted by southward distance.

"Down here . . . southerly."

Amos said: "Ahhhh." He reined around and led the others, still in that careful walk, due south. They ceased to encounter loose stock. In fact, after ten minutes, they were no longer within rifle range of the northward area where they'd had that fight.

Everett, riding stirrup with Hugh Barnum, said: "Danged horse must've run off with him to get this far away."

Hugh knew better. "Not that horse. I broke that horse myself. He'd never run off with nobody."

Mick, listening to these comments, came up with his own notion. "Chased someone down here more'n likely."

"Well, hell, I didn't figure there was more'n five of 'em," said Barnum.

Mick shrugged and made no comment about this. Hugh usually came up with protests like that; it pained him clear to the marrow to be wrong about things. Mick knew this and had learned to live with it. He didn't particularly care for Hugh Barnum, neither did Everett, but when you were the last ones hired on, you kept your dog-goned counsel to yourself.

"Yonder he is," said Amos. "On foot."

Everett pushed up even with Amos and squinted ahead with his younger and therefore better eyes. "Hey, by golly, he ain't alone."

All four of them came up onto Vern Howten wearing strong scowls of concentration. Amos reined down and leaned upon his hands where they lay over the saddle horn. Vern was standing beside someone much shorter than he was, rumpled and loosely dressed and defiant. At his feet lay a softly groaning man who kept rocking himself back and forth in the pewter grass.

"How'd you do it?" Amos asked, studying those two captive horse thieves, evidently a little dumb-founded that prisoners could have been taken after that fierce, slashing attack.

"Shot the horse out from under this scrawny

one. Winged the other one as he was busting up, blazing away at me. He got my animal, but I busted his hip . . . or busted something down there anyway, maybe only a leg. Anyway, he cart-wheeled out of the saddle, his horse kept right on going, and here I was with two live ones."

Amos's long, lipless mouth slowly closed, slowly hardened into an unrelenting, bloodless slash across his lower face. For a while he considered the standing rustler, got back that same fierce look of complete defiance, then he turned with unmistakable purpose and ran his uncompromising stare northward, southward, and finally eastward where a bosque of wind-tortured old cottonwood trees stood.

"Those trees'll do," he said. "Mick, you and Everett get that other one onto his feet and fetch him along to the cottonwoods."

Amos turned, kneed his horse, and went riding slowly across to where those ancient trees stood with their spotty, white trunks looking bleached and bone-like in dawn's weak and watery, uncertain light. He took down his lariat, selected a jutting big limb, tossed the rope over, and dismounted to catch the swinging slipknot end.

The wounded rustler fainted when Mick and Everett hauled him upright. His companion walked along between Vern and Hugh Barnum like someone in a trance, like a sleepwalker whose limbs moved mechanically but all of whose other senses had been frozen into numbness.

Mick and Everett had the hardest time of it. That one with the broken leg or shattered hip—no one ever bothered to determine which it was—sagged through their arms like a wet sack of grain. They finally took hold of his two hands and dragged him. He bumped along as though he were already dead.

Amos stepped up to peer downward when Mick let go and Everett also stepped away. "Ain't dead, is he?" Amos asked sharply.

Hugh Barnum bent far down, hung that way a moment, then straightened up wagging his head. "Out, is all," Hugh reported. "Probably from the pain."

Amos said: "You got a canteen, Hugh. Pour water over him while we're caring for this other one."

Hugh walked back toward his horse.

Vern took the slipknot end of Amos's rope, snugged it roughly around the gullet of the smallest rustler, flipped the slack, and nodded. Amos took the loose end back to his horse with him. He mounted, took two overlapping dallies around the horn, turned the animal, and went riding off westward. Once, the horse had to dig in, had to drop his head and throw his weight into that rearward drag as the lariat cut down hard into soft cottonwood fiber. After that, for a little

24

while, there was a wild whipping of the rearward rope. This, though, gradually diminished.

Amos sat up there, holding his dallies. He sat a little sideways, twisted from the waist, looking backward. Hugh Barnum had emptied his canteen over the fainted man with some success. But when that injured man was hoisted up, turned for Vern to adjust the second lariat, and he saw that infrequently convulsing small figure above him, he let off a high-pitched scream that set every-one's teeth on edge, and flung himself about wildly for a moment, then sagged down in another faint.

Barnum looked inquiringly out where old Amos was sitting. So did Vern. Amos bobbed his head up and down.

"Go ahead," he ordered. "Let's get this done. If we fetched him around, he'd probably just faint again anyway."

Mick and Everett supported the limp rustler again while Vern took Barnum's horse, took his dallies, and slowly rode out even with old Amos. This time there was no fierce struggling. The second rustler simply turned gently from side to side.

Amos, keeping his slack taut, rode far out and around the cottonwood tree; he made three of those turns before casting off his dallies for Hugh Barnum to make the rope fast to the trunk.

Several minutes later Vern did the same thing.

Hugh made the second rope fast with his back to those gently turning dawn-lit, grisly figures up there. Afterward he did as Mick and Everett also did; he walked out to climb up behind Vern without once looking back. Amos led out northward.

No one said a word until, sometime later, Amos turned and gruffly ordered Mick and Everett to go rope a mount for Vern out of the scattered remuda grazing round-about in this eerie, new day's first light.

The sun was not yet risen, the land lay under a kind of blighted grayness, the distant mountains were still, in their crumpled cañons, holding back some of that former nighttime sootiness, but along the eastern crust of the world a faint and persevering pastel shade of pale, steely blue steadily widened.

This night was now ended; for better or for worse nothing that had happened could ever be undone. The world would move along, men's lives would spin out, but everything that had been done was now frozen forever in time, unchangeable, unalterable.

Chapter Three

Amos McCarthy's Rafter M Ranch covered sixty-three hundred acres of deeded land, but because it completely surrounded three major springs—called water holes—precluding their use by others, his total acreage was closer to ten thousand acres.

The main ranch lay along Firewood Creek within sight of the forested hills out of which Firewood Creek came boiling and brawling.

Rafter M's buildings were old, and except for one shack—Amos's original sod house—they were sturdily constructed of peeled, notched logs. The way those buildings had been placed put one in mind of circled-up wagons. This was no accident either, for when old Amos had come to upland Wyoming, the Ute, Blackfeet, Dakota, and Cheyenne Indians had still ruled. Their bronco braves had roamed this land with guns and fire arrows, and the only way a man survived was to out-Indian the Indians.

Amos had been a young stalwart in those days, as big and powerful as any Indian buck, as willing to fight and as crafty at it, too. Before the Indian nations had been swept away, in their smoky lodges, around their hunting fires, in their night-time haunts, they told tales of this terrible white man, and later, in the sundown of their time when the buffalo were gone and they starved, only the foolish and the very desperate killed Rafter M beef, because Amos and his fighting riders made it a particular point to track down every Indian who did this, and Amos's variety of punishment was the one kind of death Indians shrank from— hanging. A hanged man, Indians believed, lost his soul and could therefore never enter the Great Sand Hills but must forever wander in the darkness of a half world.

When the Indians were driven from their ancient homeland, others came to make forays against Rafter M beef and horses. Amos's methods did not change. He realized as well as all the uplands cowmen did, that in a land where the law was distant and often indifferent, the surest way to inspire respect among outlaws and thieves was to be implacable in pursuit and emphatic in punish-ment.

It worked as well with white men as with red men. Until that moonlit night when rustlers had hit his horse herd, thirty days before he and his men wiped out the outlaws on their second raid, Amos McCarthy had not been bothered in two years. That was quite a record in a country where lawlessness was rampant and where hard-riding soldiers, sheriffs, and U.S. marshals could not begin to patrol all of it because the country was too large, too mountainous, and too wild.

Lynching rustlers was common practice. Although it was not legal in the strictest sense, it was nevertheless tacitly condoned by those harassed lawmen. A cowman was expected to report it, but not many did. The usual practice was to hang the rustlers, then bury them, and close one's mind as well as one's lips, thereby accomplishing what had to be done with a minimum of aftermath.

This was the best way. It was not uncommon for a man to report a lynching, ride on home, and perhaps within a week, a month, a year, have a stranger ride into his yard on a black night, hail the house from his saddle, and when the rancher opened his door with lamplight behind him, to be shot and killed, his assassin afterward racing away into the darkness never to be identified or apprehended.

It was very unlikely, as in Amos's case, that seven rustlers could be killed, without some of them at least having vengeful relatives. That was why Amos ambled into Rafter M's log bunkhouse the night after the battle, poured himself a tin cup of black java, eased down at the big room's one old table, and told his riders that nothing that happened under that big yellow moon must ever be mentioned by any of them.

"We done right," he rumbled, looking stolidly down into his cup of coffee. "But I've seen a heap of men die and I never yet took no satisfaction from having a hand in it. Someday, folks say, we'll have enough law to take care of these things, but I know for a fact that day ain't arrived yet, so us fellers that live now . . . not twenty years from now . . . we do what's got to be done, even though it haunts a man for a little while." Amos drained off the coffee, put the cup aside, and ranged his sunken gaze over the others. "And if we're smart, we never talk about it to anyone. That is, if we want to go on living, we don't, because them fellers got friends and relatives somewhere who'd want to avenge 'em." Amos stood up. "You understand, boys?"

Hugh Barnum said: "We understand, Mister Amos."

Mick and Everett and Vern Howten, over by the cook stove, gravely nodded but none of them spoke.

Amos considered those three for a moment. "Vern, take Mick and Everett back down there tomorrow in a wagon. Take shovels and crowbars. All right?"

Howten mumbled assent. Every one of them understood that those three would bury the dead, drag brush over the graves, and that would be the end of it.

Barnum, already thinking beyond this, said: "What about them horses they run off the first time? That was thirty head of mighty good stock."

"Forget it," replied old Amos. "We got plenty of

good horses. Most likely them horses are scattered from hell to breakfast by now." He drew in a big breath and let it out. "They paid for 'em, Hugh. They paid as high a price as men can pay for thieving off other folks."

Vern finished at the stove, crossed to the table, and dropped down there, his swarthy face partly in shadows, his dark, expressionless eyes solemn and thoughtful. "There were too many not to have someone coming around asking questions. They came from somewhere, Amos. Other folks saw 'em, talked to 'em probably. Maybe even knew they were heading up this way."

McCarthy nodded. "I been thinking of that, too, Vern. That's why I come out here tonight, reminding you boys that silence is plumb golden from now on. In the old days you'd catch a bronco buck, or maybe a pair of rustlers. In those times outlaws moved by stealth, so when you killed 'em and socked 'em away, no one ever knew. But like you just said, nowadays rustlers travel pretty open. They talk to folks, cut a big swathe in the towns. They're as bold as a wolf in a sheep pen."

Amos said no more for a while. He watched Mick Gleason pour a cup of coffee, hand it to Everett Tarr, and pour himself another cup. He said: "So that's how it's got to be from now on, lads. And one more thing . . . if you see any strangers on our range, let me know right away.

We've got to be on our guard. Maybe nothing'll come of this, but it don't pay not to be prepared . . . ever. Good night."

After Amos left, Vern bent, tugged off his boots, and sat staring at them. Hugh Barnum went over and drained the coffee pot. Mick walked to his wall bunk, eased down there, and sipped coffee. Everett Tarr, still over by the cook stove, said quietly: "It must be hard . . . living in that big old house all alone like Amos does . . . especially on nights like this when a feller's got unpleasant things on his mind."

"He's used to it," responded Barnum. "I've heard tales about old Amos that'd curl your hair. He even had the damned Injuns scairt to death of him. Naw, he'll go to bed, close his eyes, and sleep like a baby."

Vern Howten swung, put a cold look on Hugh, remained that way for a while, evidently near to saying something caustic, then looked away without ever saying it.

"But he's sure right," stated Everett. "It'd be wise, if after tonight we never even talked about that fight among ourselves. Just closed our minds to it altogether."

Mick agreed with this and nodded, looking over at Everett from across the rim of his coffee cup. When he drained the thing, got up, and padded over to drop it into the wash bucket, he said: "If no strangers show up asking questions within a year, I figure the thing'll pretty well die out by itself after that. How about it, Vern?"

"A year is a mighty long time, Mick. It'll seem more like five years before it's over. But you're right. If no one comes nosing around by next spring . . ." Vern stood up, shrugged, and began unbuttoning his shirt.

Hugh Barnum said: "I don't envy you boys going back down there tomorrow."

Everett Tarr put an assessing look upon Barnum; it seemed that Hugh always managed to say the wrong thing. Everett told himself not everyone was born with that knack. He went to his bunk, kicked off his boots, and sat down. He wagged his head, still thinking ironically of Hugh Barnum. It was almighty hard to like a man like Barnum.

"Good thing it's still cold," said Barnum, pursuing his same grisly train of thought. "If it was mid August, they'd be swollen up like poisoned gophers after being out there two days. And the smell . . ."

"Shut up," growled Vern Howten. "You got about as much tact as a bear. Go to bed, Hugh."

"Well, hell," complained Barnum, "I was just thinking out loud is all, Vern."

"Well, don't. Think all you want, only do it in silence."

Mick turned toward Everett, winked, and stood up to undress, to strip down to his long-handled red flannel underwear, which doubled for nightclothes. Across the way Howten got down under his blankets, lay back with both arms under his head, gazing steadily out the front window where the same yellow old moon, which had been overhead two nights before, was serenely crossing a purple sky. A corner of that moon seemed to have been shaved off a little and some of its brightness had diminished. Mick was the last one into bed so he had to go over and blow down the lamp chimney, putting out the coal-oil lamp.

For a little while the four of them lay in silence; they might have been sleeping except that something was there in the shared gloom keeping them all awake.

"Vern?" a voice quietly said from the silent dark.

"Yeah?"

"You ever done that before?"

"Go to sleep, Tarr."

"I want an answer. You ever been in on a thing like that before?"

"That's none of your cussed business, Tarr."

"All right, I'll put it another way. Does the law get interested when it hears there's been a hanging like that?"

"You heard Amos. Even Mick said the best thing is for us never to mention it again. If we don't talk about it, the chances of the law ever knowing anything are just about nil."

"Listen, Vern," said Everett with abrupt intentness. "I don't know whether you're that simple or not . . . but I ain't. What I want to know is whether a man ought to saddle up and ride out while he's got the chance, or not."

Vern's voice turned tired-sounding when he answered this. "Every man's got to make his own decisions and you're no exception, Everett. You got all night to figure it out."

Tarr was briefly silent, then he said: "Mick, what do you think?"

"I think I'm sleepy," mumbled Gleason. "Quit talking, Ev."

Out of the northward corner back by the cook stove Hugh Barnum's voice came, saying: "You fellers better be sure and take crowbars with you tomorrow. That ground down there's rocky as all get out, and you'll want to plant 'em plenty deep so's the cussed wolves don't dig 'em up. That could be embarrassing . . . having riders come onto their carcasses scattered around after wolves dug 'em up."

Vern swore, his voice both fierce and roughened by temper. "Hugh, one more word out of you and I'm going to yank you out of those blankets and stomp the wadding out of you. Now the bunch of you . . . dammit . . . go to sleep!"

Nothing more was said; the bunkhouse was as still as a tomb except for a little whimpering wind that worried eaves and loose roof shakes. The softly lit yard with its gray, log buildings was steeped in a kind of sad and lonely stillness. The moon went down gradually, swinging with eternal grace toward the same timeless stiffly standing mountain tops and silver snow fields it had crossed over since the world began, and a long way off two limp silhouettes turned half around and half back again, suspended as they were from a cottonwood limb.

Chapter Four

Vern drove while Mick and Everett sat in the bed of the wagon idly talking, idly smoking. They left Rafter M about sunup and went eastward for two miles, then south for another mile and a half before they came upon the first pair. They were the ones old Amos had cut down while Mick and Everett had been riding with him.

While Mick and Everett dug, Vern went back and got that one with the two punctures in him, the first one put there by Tarr, the second one pumped into his prone body by Amos as he'd jumped his horse over the man.

And Barnum had been right about the ground, too; it was as hard as iron and chock-full of those round niggerhead boulders. Mick and Everett had the graves knee-deep by the time Vern returned with the bouncing, lifeless body. They halted, using Vern's return as an excellent excuse to halt, drink deeply from canteens, and afterward have a thoughtful smoke.

"Damned grave looks like a trench," muttered Mick.

"If we'd made three separate ones," Everett retorted, "we'd be digging in this confounded earth until next week."

Vern walked over, looked in, shook his head, and walked back. "Got to be at least twelve inches deeper," he pronounced.

They all looked at one another, each remembering Barnum's words of the night before but unwilling to mention them, or Hugh Barnum, either, for that matter. Mick and Everett went back to digging. Vern pulled the corpse from the wagon, rolled it over beside the other two, and stood there distastefully smoking and keeping his eyes everywhere but downward.

"You two are sure slow," he said.

Mick straightened up, red-faced and hostile. "If you can do better, hop to it."

Nothing more was said until the trench was finished, the bodies rolled over to the edge of it ready to be pushed in, then Everett suddenly threw out a hand restraining Vern Howten from using his boot toe to dump the first rustler. "Better search 'em first, hadn't we, Vern?"

Howten looked grim when he shook his head. "Bury whatever they got on 'em, right along with 'em."

Everett was aghast. "Watches," he said, "and maybe money?"

"Everything," Vern growled, put his toe against a body, and shoved. "Roll them others in, too, Mick."

"Hey, what the hell sense does this make," protested Everett. "If they got maybe a hundred dollars between them, ain't it better we should spend it than that it should molder in the ground like this?"

Vern's black eyes flashed with abrupt exasperation. "Ev, you listen to me. That big one there's got a gold watch. I know he has because I saw it. That one over by your foot's got a gold signet ring on, too. Now suppose someone come asking around about these men and you said you'd never seen 'em or heard of 'em . . . and had that signet ring on. Or maybe Mick was telling time by that gold watch when someone saw the thing? You get the point, Everett? Then, damn you, shut up and roll that one in!"

Mick was between those two. He did not look at either of them; he simply trundled his dead man over the lip of the grave, down into it, and jerked back at the sound that corpse made as it struck hard earth. He looked over at Vern and nodded, then he looked around at Everett. "Give him a little shove," he said. Everett sullenly obeyed, and they afterward filled the trench, cut brush, and dragged it back and forth until all indication that a grave was underfoot was quite obliterated.

Vern gathered the tools, tossed them into the

wagon, climbed wordlessly to the seat, and clucked at the team. Mick and Everett swung up over the tailgate, sat there side-by-side looking solemnly back, saying nothing, and on all sides of them a still, bright, and clean-appearing world lay blandly as though no fight had taken place, no men had violently died, and no grave had been dug, filled, and left behind.

They found the next two and hauled them around behind a scrub-oak clump where there was shade to bury them. Here, Vern Howten came down from his long, grim silence. He even spelled off Mick and Everett at the digging. If this made taciturn Vern feel better, it made Everett and Mick feel much better. At the other trench they'd felt like outcasts of some kind. Maybe Vern had also felt that way back there; at any rate he was different as they measured their second oblong hole and he pronounced it deep enough.

This time it was much easier; they simply drove the wagon up close, snaked the bodies out, and rolled them into their pit, and commenced shoveling in dirt. They shoveled, rested, talked a little, and shoveled some more. When it had been finished, the earth was tamped and dragged to hide the grave. They loaded up, drove a half mile southward toward their final destination, halted behind a little land swell, and smoked, drank cold water, and drowsed for a little while, desultorily talking about cattle drives, horses they had known, everything under the sun but that final chore left to do before they turned homeward in the reddening afternoon.

Vern said: "That damned Barnum. There are times when I could slit his ear and yank his arm through it."

"Yeah," muttered Mick. "I've known fellers like that before. They ought to make peppermint-flavored boots for 'em. Every damned time they open their mouths, they put their foot into it. Take last night now . . ." Mick heaved a big ragged sigh. "He just had to keep on talking."

Everett straightened up, thumbed back his hat, and ran a long look out and around. "Why does Amos keep him anyway? Man, I've been on a dozen ranches where they'd cut him out and send him packing the first week."

"He's the best there is with horses," offered Vern. "Maybe sometime Nature does that with fellers . . . gives 'em a special gift, then leaves something else out of their make-up."

"Well, she sure left something out of him," agreed Mick, also straightening up. He cocked an assessing eye skyward. "We'd better get along and get this over with. It'll be long after supper by the time we get back, as it is."

Vern climbed back to the seat, lifted the lines, and flicked them. The team leaned, the wagon jerked, steel tires ground down into flinty soil, and they were borne out around the land swell, almost at once coming in view of that burdened cotton-wood tree. Neither Mick nor Everett saw it because their backs were to the wagon's front, but Vern did. He had to drive nearly a mile with those two puffy, suspended figures straight before him. By the time he eased back on the lines, his face was set like iron in an unpleasant expression and he had lapsed back into his customary dogged, harsh silence.

All he said when they stopped was: "Dig here!"

Mick and Everett looked up, looked down, and dug. For a long time there was only the sound of steel striking hardpan, then more rocks, the same rounded, smooth stones that had been encountered at the other burial sites.

Vern walked out a ways to cut brush and drag it back. He kept his head down as did the other two. Time ran on, the afternoon waned, golden sunlight reddened, shadows began to appear on the east side of the cottonwoods out beyond the wagon and the team.

Mick raised up in the hole, looked at all four squared corners, heaved out his crowbar, his shovel, put both hands palms down upon the crumbly bank, and sprang up. He turned to hold a hand forth to Everett, grunting as he yanked his pardner up out of that hole.

"Dryer'n a bone," croaked Everett, pushing on past where the canteens hung. Mick followed him.

Vern paced over, squinted into the hole, found

it satisfactory, and paced back to the wagon, heaved up onto the seat, and clucked the team around, bringing the rig directly under those two forlorn shapes overhead. He could have ordered Mick or Everett to stand up on that high seat and cut the ropes, but he didn't. He got up there himself, clumsily opened his Barlow knife, set his face to the work ahead, reached far up, and slashed.

The first body to fall slackly into the wagon bed was that of the rustler Vern had shot in the hip. His hat fell off and one arm draped itself over the sideboard.

Everett and Mick stopped drinking, capped their canteens, and stood like stone watching Vern inch along his high perch to cut down the second body.

Out of nowhere a little breeze came limping along bending the grass, making it dance and writhe. Vern looked up, raised his hand, and slashed at the second hard-twist lariat rope. This one, with less weight at the end of it, frayed but did not break. Vern uttered a strangled curse and slashed again, harder this time. The rope parted. That second body dropped like a stone striking the wagon, and again a hat rolled off.

Mick looked away, out and around and back again. "Ev," he said, "you got any tobacco?"

Everett had. They both went to work manufacturing smokes unmindful of Vern up there on the wagon seat, unmindful of the grisly job now to be performed, unmindful of everything, in fact, for this little length of time, but the business of deeply inhaling, deeply exhaling.

There was not a sound anywhere. Mick twisted to look off into the reddening west. Everett also turned his back. They meant to stand that way evidently, until Vern clucked at the team and drove out, around, and back up beside the fresh, raw grave. But Vern didn't do that. They waited with their cigarettes half smoked for the creak and rattle and it never came. Finally Mick turned.

Vern was still standing up there on the seat. He was rigid up there, his dark, swarthy face pale from lips to forehead, staring hard down into the wagon bed below him.

Mick softly said: "Come on, Vern. This is the end of it. Pull around here and let's get this over with."

Vern might not have heard. He remained up there incongruously stiff and tall atop the wagon seat. Everett squinted up into Vern's face.

"What's wrong?" he softly asked. "Vern, what the hell's wrong with you?"

At last Howten spoke. He turned his head the slightest bit, gazed out of a horrified face down where the others stood, and said: "Come over here you two. Look down into this god-damned wagon."

Everett, shocked by the range boss' frightful expression, stood rooted and staring upward, but

Mick dropped his smoke, stepped on it, and moved out. He crossed over, halted where he could see inward and downward, went as rigid as Vern had been, and Everett heard his breath go out in a rattling, long rush.

"God Almighty," Mick said. "Good God Almighty."

You didn't ride with a man, share blankets and campfires with him as long as Everett had with Mick Gleason, and not know what every inflexion of his voice meant. Everett looked briefly at Mick's stiff shoulders, flung aside his smoke, too, and went up to the wagon side in five long strides, forewarned by the horror in his pardner's tone but not prepared for what he saw.

"It's a girl."

When the second hanged rustler's hat had fallen off, a wealth of taffy-yellow hair had tumbled out in cascading waves around the sightless, wide-open blue eyes.

"Great God in heaven, Mick, it's a girl!"

Everett's jerked-out pronouncement acted as a trigger on Vern Howten. He slumped, shook himself, turned, and groped down off the wagon seat to the ground. There, he put his back to a fore wheel and leaned, all limp and listless, staring far out westerly.

Mick stepped back, turned, and walked as far as the nearest cottonwood tree. He put his hand upon the trunk as though for support and kept his back to the others, to the wagon, and to the grave they'd dug.

Everett also moved off, but he kept looking from one of his companions to the other, and swallowing. Finally he said: "How did it happen? Vern, you caught these two . . . didn't you know? Didn't she speak so's you'd know from her voice?"

Howten shook his head without speaking. He looked like a man on the verge of being actively ill.

"Mick? Mick?"

"What?"

"How did it happen?"

"Ev, it was dark. You were there, you know. It was dark and neither of 'em said anything. Maybe she was stunned from her fall. I don't know."

"But I know," said Vern finally, his face ghastly, his voice hoarse and unsteady. "We done it too fast. That's why it happened. I remember something, too. That other one . . . the one I shot in the leg . . . when he came to and seen . . . her . . . kicking out her life up there. You remember? He flung himself around like a wild man. He whimpered, and then he fainted. You remember?"

They remembered but neither of them said so. Over by the cottonwood tree Mick pushed upright, dropped that supporting arm, and turned to look back at the other two.

"You're right, Vern, we did it too fast. Amos

had the rope ready. He went through the whole thing like an old hand at it."

"He *is* an old hand at it, boys," Vern murmured. "He's hung more Injuns for horse-stealing than you can shake a stick at. He's socked away plenty of white rustlers, too. But . . . God Almighty . . . !"

Mick rallied first. He started back with that dying-day redness upon his face and across his shoulders. "We've got to bury 'em. Come on."

Chapter Five

It was near 10:00 p.m. when the wagon ground into Rafter M's yard. Its three grim passengers took their time at the unharnessing, at turning out the team, forking them feed, and checking the water trough.

The bunkhouse was dark, but over at the main house a lamp still shone orange in the pit of the night. That yellow old moon was just rising over some ghostly peaks far out, its glow subdued, its roundness uneven.

Mick and Everett came together near the barn's doorless front opening, waiting for Vern who was still down with the wagon. It took a long time for Vern to put away the crowbars and shovels but eventually he came along. He didn't say anything, only stood there with the other two gazing across where that yellow light shone squarely, its glow puddling down across the main house front verandah out into the still, melancholy night.

"Well," stated Vern quietly. "Amos is still up, and that's good. He's got to be told."

Mick and Everett stood still, waiting for Vern to make the first move. He did. He started onward in a shuffling way.

The three of them got across to the porch, paused a moment there, then stepped up over rough planking, their boot falls sounding hollow, sounding inordinately loud in the night. Vern knocked and stepped back, looking patient and resigned and brooding in the gloom.

Old Amos came to the door, opened it, and peered out. His mane of tousled white hair shone like silver in the light behind him. His longhorn mustache drooped. He looked bigger, more raw-boned, more unkempt than usual.

"So you're back," he said matter-of-factly. "All right, boys. Turn in."

When none of those three made a move, Amos pushed his head out a little in a thrusting way, his eyes jumped from face to face, resettled upon Vern Howten, and lingered there. He seemed to sense something here. He had a little book in one hand, which he had evidently been reading when Vern had knuckled the front door. He turned slightly, put the book aside, and turned back again.

"It's all done, ain't it?" he asked. "No trouble was there? Dammit Vern . . . speak up, man."

Vern didn't speak but he pushed out his right hand and opened it. Something small and shiny and heart-shaped glistened in that weak light. Old Amos squinted, took the thing, and half turned again so room light would reveal whatever that object was.

"A locket," he said. "A locket like girls wear around their necks. Vern, where'd you get this thing? Didn't anyone come onto you boys at the burying, did they?"

"No," replied Vern. "I don't think anyone saw us. The locket . . . Remember the little one we hanged, the one that acted stunned or something? Well, Amos, that one was a girl."

Amos came back around very slowly, his craggy old face turning incredulous. He blinked out at Mick, at Everett, back down at the little locket in his hand. "No," he whispered. "It couldn't be."

"It was. I took that locket off her just before we dumped her in the hole. Look inside, Amos . . . there's initials in there."

But Amos ignored this last. "It couldn't be," he said again, his voice scarcely audible. "How come, Vern? What was a girl doing with rustlers in the night like that?"

Vern shrugged and turned silent.

Mick said: "Maybe the wife of one of 'em. Remember how that one Vern shot in the hip

48

went sort of crazy when he come to and saw her hanging up there convulsing?"

Amos kept staring at the locket for a long time before he stepped aside, jerked his head for the others to enter, then closed the door behind them, closed his fist over the locket, and strode over where a bottle of rye whiskey stood upon a littered table. With his back to Vern and Mick and Everett, he poured a stiff drink, downed it neat, coughed, and turned back.

"Have a drink," he told the others. "There's glasses here."

While the cowboys were pouring, old Amos went across to a blackened big stone fireplace and planted his legs wide apart. He bent a little, put his hand near the table lamp over there, gradually opened his hand, and stared at that little heart-shaped golden locket. He fumbled at opening it; his thumbnail was too thick, so he dug out a pocket knife and used the thinner blade to pry back one half of the locket.

"N.J.," he muttered. "N.J. from H.J."

Vern nodded. "There's a date, too, Amos."

Mick and Everett had their straight shots of that rye whiskey. It had been a long time since breakfast; gradually the world began to become a warmer, more orderly place again. They sauntered away from the table, found chairs, and dropped down, watching old Amos bending from the waist and scowling at that shining locket he held.

Vern stayed at the table; he had himself a second belt before corking the bottle. He belched, ignored this, and said: "I pulled her rope up."

Amos ignored this remark, closed the locket, turned it over and over, examining it, straightened up finally, and dropped the thing into a vest pocket. He was half in light, half in shadow near that blackened stone fireplace. Lamplight coming from down below struck against his prominent jaw, upward, and this cast his higher features in an unnatural shadowy gloom. He seemed larger than life, all gaunt and grim-visaged.

"We got to keep this among the four of us," he said. "I never heard of rustlers having their women along with 'em before, but that's not important now." He dropped his gaze, raked each of those three range men with it, and let his slash of a mouth draw out stubbornly thin. "It's one thing to hang horse-stealing men. It's something else again to hang girls. I don't give a damn how guilty she was . . . and every one of us in this room knows she was as damnably guilty as the others . . . she was still a female. No one'd overlook that. Not even the other cowmen."

"It was an accident," offered Vern.

"Yes, but that changes nothing. How would we ever explain an accident like that? You know what folks would say? They'd say we shouldn't have yanked 'em up without finding out who they were."

"Well," muttered Everett Tarr, "we did go about it sort of hasty, Mister McCarthy."

Amos's bleak stare dropped at once to Everett. "Everyone goes about a hanging sort of hasty, Everett. You ever hear of anyone who liked to drag it out?"

"I've never been in anything like this before. I wouldn't know how folks react."

"But you damned well know what folks'll say if they ever find out about this hanging, don't you?"

Everett looked long at his right leg, which was crossed over his left, and nodded.

"There's been a dozen rustlers hung in these uplands by other cowmen that I know of, which means probably three dozen been lynched I *don't* know of. But those same cowmen would turn against us in a minute, if they ever even heard it hinted that we hanged a girl."

Vern said quietly: "Yeah, guilty or not she was a girl. Lord, I liked to have fainted when her hat rolled off. It was like getting kicked square in the belly by a mule."

"Have another drink, Vern. And you two . . . Mick and Everett . . . you listen to me now. As long as you live don't never breathe a word of this to anyone, because if you do, you'll be ruined right along with the rest of us."

Mick and Everett sat there saying nothing. The whiskey was wearing off; the world was becoming a haunted place again.

51

Vern finished his third drink, cleared his pipes, and said: "One other thing. Barnum doesn't know."

"And you're not to tell him, either. Hugh's got his uses, boys, but he's got no more sense about when to talk and when not to than the man in the moon."

"Maybe he'll talk about the fight anyway. He was there, Mister McCarthy," said Mick. "He made the ropes fast to the tree trunk, too."

"Well, that's different. That was simply a lynching of rustlers. But I don't think he'll spill what he knows about that anyway. He was in it with the rest of us, and Hugh's no simpleton. Only don't tell him about that girl. Him or anyone else, you understand?"

Mick nodded. "We understand." He waited for Amos to say more. When Amos didn't, Mick got up out of his chair and stood, looking at the others. Everett also arose.

"How," murmured swarthy Vern Howten, looking out of swimming, dark eyes, "did she come to be there? How come none of us lookrf to see she was a girl? It stays in my mind. I can see her face now, like it was in the moonlight, as plain as day. Didn't anyone suspect it was a girl? Amos, you should've seen her face. It was pretty, even dead like she was. She couldn't have been over maybe eighteen or nineteen. Her hair was the color of . . ."

"Shut up," snapped old Amos. "Get away from

that whiskey bottle, Vern, dammit." Amos was breathing heavily now; it was as though he had a bad premonition, as though he knew that no matter what he said or did, this terrible thing was going to leak out. He stood there with his granite face plunged in evil shadows, his heavy mane of white hair awry, and his fierce mustache drooping, looking savage and badly troubled.

"Go on to bed," he said. "Don't wake Hugh up, if you can help it. By morning all of us'll be nearer to normal again. Vern, tomorrow take the boys over to Salt Valley and look for those calvy first-calf heifers. Take a come-along with you in case there's some calves got to be pulled. And, Vern, when the others come back, you stay up there at the line camp. I'll come up day after tomorrow and spell you off. All right. Good night now."

Amos crossed to the door, opened it, and stood stiffly as the three riders filed out. He looked long into each face, into Vern Howten's face hardest, and afterward very gently closed the door.

The three of them were approaching the bunkhouse steps when that light up at the main house winked out, leaving only melancholy moonlight faintly to brighten the yard.

Vern hung back, saying: "You fellers go on in. I got to take a little walk. See you in the morning."

Mick and Everett watched the range boss start along none too steadily toward the barn. Neither of them had taken more than one drink up at the main house so they were both stone sober.

As Vern faded out in night shadows, Everett took out his tobacco sack, bent his head, and said: "Never saw liquor hit him like that before. Here, you want to make a smoke?"

Mick accepted the makings and also went to work twisting up a cigarette. They both lit off the same match. "Never saw anything affect him like that, you mean," corrected Mick, making his shrewd syllepsis. "He's always been like the old man, hard as nails and rough as rock. Ev, you don't reckon there's been a girl somewhere in his past that looked like *that* one, do you?"

"I wouldn't know. All I can say for sure right now is that I ain't the least bit sleepy . . . and I wish we were a thousand miles away from here."

"Yeah, me, too. I got a bad feeling about this, Ev."

"Mick, how do you expect she came to be there like that? She was one of 'em, no getting around that. Did you ever hear of a lady rustler before?"

"No, and I wish to hell I hadn't this time, too. Amos was sure right about one thing. Folks'll raise hell and prop it up if they ever find out what we done down there."

Everett considered the flaky tip of his cigarette for a thoughtful moment, then said very softly: "You know what I think? I think you and me better take our bedrolls and get out of this country."

Mick was a long time commenting on this. He

smoked, he looked up at the ancient sky, he brought his gaze down and around to Amos's darkened house, then back to the barn area where Vern Howten had disappeared. "Maybe you're right," he eventually murmured. "One thing's dang' sure, Ev. If we hang around here, things ain't going to get any better."

"That's right. That's how I'm thinking right now. And I keep wondering about Vern. If he was to start brooding and drinking at the same time . . ." Everett didn't finish this; he didn't have to. Mick understood and nodded.

"Maybe you are right, Ev. The more I think of it, the more I believe you are. The smart thing's to get out of this upland country."

Tarr pinched out his cigarette, dropped it, and sighed aloud. "It takes a while to get used to living with something like that," he murmured.

"Like what?"

"Looking down into the cussed wagon bed and seeing her lying there. Vern's way wouldn't work for me. I could drink myself silly and she'd still be there behind my eyeballs. If I live to be a hundred, I'll never forget that, Mick."

"Won't any of us, Ev, but for the sake of my continued health, I'm sure going to try."

Mick went over closer to the bunkhouse door, hesitated at the sight of a wispy dark shadow emerging from the barn, and said: "Come on. Let's hit the hay. We'll talk about this leaving business tomorrow." He pushed on into the bunkhouse.

Ev also saw Vern in the shank of the night, only he didn't study him as pensively as Mick had before he, too, passed on inside, because Ev had made his decision. He was like that; once Everett adopted an idea, it was the same as accomplished in his mind; he would not abandon it, particularly an idea like this one that was so crystal clear. If they remained at Rafter M, no good would come of it. If they left, the past would be definitely behind them.

Chapter Six

Vern didn't give Hugh Barnum much time to ask questions the following morning, and if he attributed the moroseness of Vern or the pre-occupation of Mick and Everett to anything, it must have been to the fact that since they hadn't returned until very late the night before and had to arise again at 5:00 this morning, they were grumpy over this and nothing else.

The four of them rode out of the yard north-bound some time before the sun came up. They were skirting the foothills when that faint first red blush brightened their insular world, riding quietly along in a westerly way with the mountains on their right.

It was pleasant all the way to Salt Valley, which

was actually the bottom of a prehistoric lake or crater completely surrounded by forested slopes. There was rich soil here, and, out almost in the valley's exact center, there was a small, clear-water lake.

Here, Amos had been salting his cattle for thirty years. Here, too, was evidence that for a long, long time before Amos McCarthy or anyone like him had ever seen Salt Valley, Indians had rendezvoused here, built camps, lived and died, safe from natural and human enemies.

There was one trail into Salt Valley from Rafter M. Vern led the way through giant pines over a carpet of needles so thick it was spongy. He was his usual self, too, all the way down to where cattle grazed, dark red and greasy fat, saying nothing, looking darkly Indian-like, slouching along in the saddle with philosophical resignation, the come-along tied aft of his cantle, a spare lariat lashed to the left-hand swell of his Miles City saddle.

Rock salt glowed like snow crystals where Hugh had dumped it here ten days before. The ground for a hundred feet around that lick was churned into powdery dust. There were cattle standing there as those four horsemen came down out of the trees; they threw up their faces in alarm, but after a while, when those riders ignored them, the critters relaxed again, following the mounted men with their eyes.

Twenty years earlier old Amos had put two handy cowboys to erecting a log line shack at Salt Valley. No one remembered those riders at all, but their handiwork stood now as solid and ingeniously contrived as the day they'd finished it. The walls were immensely thick, competently chinked with straw-mixed mud, and at first glance one got the impression that nothing short of a cannonball could have dented the little building. Out back was a corral of peeled poles, but obviously this had been erected much later.

Vern made for this line shack, swung stiffly down, and hiked over to push aside the door and peer inside. Barnum, in the act of also dismounting, said: "Varmints get anything?"

Vern drew back, turned, and shook his head. No matter how tight line shacks were in the upland country, unless a man put even his canned foods in a box and suspended it from ceiling rafters, porcupines, wood rats, and sometimes foxes or coyotes, given ample time and a shrunken gut, would keep working until they got to the food.

"You want to eat first," asked Hugh, "or make a sashay?"

Vern was back beside his horse. "Mick," he said, ignoring Barnum, "you and Ev split up and ride east and west, making a sweep of the valley. Hugh, you go around to the southwest, and I'll go southeast. We'll cover the whole place that way. Watch for springing heifers. If you see any in labor or springing, fire one shot and I'll head for you with the come-along." Vern stepped up over leather, turned his horse, and added gruffly: "We'll meet back here about sundown." He and Hugh rode off together, Vern his customary taciturn self, Hugh babbling about their prospects of finding any of those calvy heifers this early in the day.

Mick, with his gaze upon Barnum's fading back, wagged his head back and forth. He and Everett cut around the line shack and split up, each heading toward the forested slopes farther out, neither one saying a word to the other.

There were quite a number of Rafter M critters in Salt Valley, which was understandable because, aside from this one spot and the home ranch, Amos put out no salt. There was a most excellent reason for this. In mountainous country, riders could work ten dozen horses to death hunting cattle that did not wish to be found, whereas one saltlick, maintained always in the same location, drew critters for miles around, and if there happened also to be plenty of clean water and good grass close by, the cattle usually did not stray far from that lick, making it relatively easy for riders to watch their movement from time to time, and later on in the fall of the year to round them up for the long drive to lower elevations.

The one constant exception to this was calving

cows. Whether they were first-calf heifers or old gummers who'd dropped maybe ten calves, these old girls invariably sought complete seclusion for the birthing, and this was why Vern had split up the Rafter M crew, sending each rider up near the forest fringe in a circling way, to ferret out any heifers whose time might be approaching, or that might be in the act of prenatal labor.

What cowmen called a come-along was simply a ratchet-handled block-and-tackle type of tool more easterly farmers used for stretching barbed-wire. Regardless of a man's physical power, his size, or even his ingenuity, there were plenty of times when none of these things, or all of them used concurrently, was sufficient to pull a big calf out of a small cow. That's when the come-along was employed; one end of its sturdy rope was made fast to a tree-trunk, a fence post, a large boulder, the other end was made fast to the hung-up calf's protruding legs—assuming the calf was coming right—and the cowboy then slowly, firmly, pumped the ratchet-handle back and forth, pulling the calf out of the cow a little at a time.

Occasionally the calf was stillborn, but more often it was alive and healthy. The thing was, if the heifer had been straining for, say, six or eight hours, which was not at all unusual, she was ordinarily too weak to have the calf without help. If no cowboy showed up, she died and so did the calf. First-calf heifers were a headache, but then, cow ranching in the upland country was never claimed by those who knew to be the easiest life on earth, so the riders made their riding rounds, hoping not to encounter difficulty in a place as large and well stocked as Salt Valley, but encountering it nonetheless.

The sun was slightly off-center when Mick found his particular heifer. She was wild as a deer, ordinarily, but now, after straining for close to fourteen hours, she only rolled sunken, bloodshot eyes, weakly shook her horns, then lay over on her side gustily breathing, resigned and indifferent, her physical pain dimming out everything else.

Mick was lucky, though. This calf was half out, the water bag had broken, and miracle of miracles, the little critter was still alive. Barely so, but nevertheless still alive.

Mick did not fire his six-gun for Vern and the come-along. He dismounted instead, took down his lariat, flipped the hondo end over the calf's legs, took two light dallies around his saddle horn, and very gently backed his horse.

He had to stop three times awaiting the contractual spasms of the gasping heifer, then he had the calf delivered. He was thinking that usually riders were not this lucky, as he slapped the calf's face and pumped his lungs. He was not thinking of anything else at all during this tense and dramatic moment when he was fighting to preserve life, so did not see the shadow of another man back a hundred feet in among the shadowy pines.

The calf bleated a quavering, wet little bawl that sounded as though his lungs might be full of fluid. Mick swung the little critter downhill; if there was fluid, it could drain out now. He got up, put a wary eye on the wicked-horned cow, saw that although she was undoubtedly relieved and worried over that little bawl, she was still not able to jump up and charge him, and turned to recoiling his lariat.

That was when his wandering gaze fell upon that still and silent man back in the trees who had obviously been watching all this, and who even more obviously was a total stranger.

Mick stopped coiling, almost stopped breathing. Everything that had just happened was erased from his mind in a second. Something sour filled his belly and remained there for as long as those two kept staring at one another.

Finally the stranger left his formless tree shadows, paced down almost to where the groaning heifer still lay, and halted again. He was a powerfully built man of Mick's own size, but much heavier. His face, though, was lean, somewhat hawk-like, and burned as brown as desert adobe. He wore an ivory-butted six-gun, had buckskin roping gloves tucked carelessly into a black leather bullet belt, and his dusty Stetson hat was far back on his head, revealing auburn hair curled close to his head that shone with an almost metallic rusty redness where the sun struck it.

This was no dude. In fact, Mick told himself shortly, this was trouble four ways from the middle if he'd ever seen it. He continued recoiling his rope. As soon as he did this, the stranger seemed to loosen a little, as though he'd been waiting for Mick to do one thing or the other, and now that Mick had decided to do the other, he could relax.

"You did that real neat," the stranger said in a soft-drawling tone of voice. "I figured the calf'd be dead."

"Yeah," agreed Mick guardedly, "me, too."

"She'd been in labor a long time."

"Yeah. I'd judge maybe all night. Pretty weak."

The stranger walked down a little closer. Mick had a better look at his face. He was a man in his thirties, his eyes were wide apart and missed nothing. There was something about him that was different; if he was a cowboy, he was one of the best. Also, if he was something else—well—he'd be one of the best of those, too, whatever those might be.

"Where's the main ranch?" he asked Mick.

"About six, eight miles east and south of here."

"You alone up here?"

"No. There are three other riders circling the valley."

"All looking for these calvy cows?"

"Yeah."

"Mind telling me your name, cowboy?"

"No, I don't mind. It's Mick Gleason."

Mick stepped over, hung the lariat from his saddle horn, turned, and said: "Mind telling me your name, mister?"

"Don't mind at all, Mick. It's Holt Jackson."

Mick lowered his head and began rummaging through pockets for a tobacco sack he knew he didn't have. His hands were shaking.

Holt Jackson. H.J.! To N.J. from H.J. Good God!

"Maybe you lost it," said the hawk-faced, sun-darkened big man, meaning the tobacco sack. "Here, have a smoke on me."

Mick accepted the makings but did not at once go to work. He stalled for time until his hands stopped shaking. "You working for Beaver or some of the others up in here?" he asked. "Hell of a big country. Riders get lost in it now and then. You're a good three miles inside Rafter M range. Not that it matters. No one cares about stuff like that up in here."

"Just rode in," said Holt Jackson. "Haven't had time to hire out to anyone yet. What'd you say the name of your outfit is?"

"Rafter M. Belongs to old Amos McCarthy. He's dang' near a fixture in these here mountains, been around here so long."

"You going to make that smoke, Mick?"

"Oh . . . yeah. Sort of startled me, seeing you standing back in those trees like that."

Mick troughed the paper, poured tobacco, folded the flap, licked the thing, closed it, and popped it between his lips at the same time passing back the makings. As he struck a match upon the top steel button of his pants, Holt Jackson began making a cigarette, too. Mick lit up and waited, then extended his hand for Jackson also to light up. They both exhaled.

Jackson lifted his gaze, running it on around Salt Valley as though looking for a notch in the skyline that would indicate a way in, and out. He ultimately brought his gaze back around to Mick.

"Rough country," he said mildly. "You know it pretty well, Mick?"

"Pretty well. I've been riding it now for a few months. It's rough up in here, but southward it levels out a lot."

"It'd have to level out a lot," said the big man wryly. "The way I came in here was over some danged high peaks."

"You came from the north?"

"Yeah. Straight up and over and down."

Mick shook his head at that. He and Everett had also traveled that route. It had been dizzily high and frightening, but at that time neither he nor Ev knew any other way in. It now occurred to him that Holt Jackson had never before been in the upland, either, and this led on to still another thought.

"You just heading south," he asked, "or looking for work?"

Jackson sucked back a deep drag off his cigarette. Mick heard the sweep of wind into the larger man's chest. Jackson put his considering gaze upon Mick and kept it there, his answer coming slow.

"Well, for the time being let's just say I'm looking around. Never been in these mountains before, but I've heard of 'em. For the time being, Mick, I'm just curious."

Mick accepted this. "If you get down around Rafter M when you're through looking around, maybe old Amos'd put you to work. Now, I got to be getting along. *Adiós*, Holt. Good trailing."

Chapter Seven

Mick rode a long mile up into the forest before stopping to get down and watch his back trail. There was no sound and no dust; Jackson was not trailing him. He went back to his horse, got aboard, and drifted on around the top end of Salt Valley, looking for Everett. When he found him, Ev was dozing beneath a giant pine tree. He cocked a drowsy eye at Mick, didn't move, and when Mick got down and hunkered there beside him, Ev said indifferently: "Find anything?"

"Pulled one calf," retorted Mick solemnly, "and met a man named Holt Jackson."

Everett's droopy lids very gradually lifted. His gaze came slowly around and hung upon Mick's solemn face. He didn't say anything for a long time, just kept staring. Eventually he said: "Holt Jackson?"

"The initials fit, Ev."

Now Everett came wide-awake. He straightened up against his tree. Mick related how he'd met Jackson. He also described him. He wound up by saying: "Ev, this one's no man to fool with. Maybe he was part of the gang and maybe he wasn't, but I'll tell you one thing . . . Rafter M's got real trouble."

"He won't find 'em. They're buried too good for that."

Mick picked up a twig, snapped it, and studied the broken ends for a while. "I'm not that optimistic, Ev. You're judging this Holt Jackson without ever seeing him. I told you he's no fool. On top of that he's got the look of a gunfighter to him." Mick dropped the twigs, got up, and turned to run a long gaze outward and downward over Salt Valley. "We'd better find Vern and tell him. You ready to go?"

"I was ready three hours ago."

"Didn't find anything, Ev?"

"Nothing. No heifers, no cows. Just one old carcass bears been eating on. Mick, where did Jackson go?"

"I don't know. The only thing I was watching was that he didn't follow me."

"Amos and Vern'll say you should have trailed him."

Mick got to his horse, mounted, and twisted in the saddle to say: "Amos and Vern can say what they want. I was thinking all the way up here to meet you, Ev. I've got a notion now's the time for us to light out of this country."

They rode down to the valley floor, cut straight across it as far as the little clear-water lake, halted there to let their animals tank up, then struck out again, heading for the line shack, neither of them with anything to say, each of them busy with his private thoughts.

Vern and Hugh Barnum had already corralled their horses and built a cooking fire at the stone ring outside the line shack. Vern looked up as Mick and Everett came riding along, but he didn't say anything. Hugh did, though; he wanted to know what luck they'd had. Mick told about pulling the calf but beyond that he had nothing more to say until he and Everett had put up their animals, hung their rigs by each lariated saddle horn high in a tree so the porcupines would not chew them to pieces in their eternal hunt for salt, sauntered back around where Vern was frying meat with potatoes, and sat down upon the line shack stoop to watch this. Then Mick told of his meeting with the stranger.

Vern listened closely with his back to Mick. He went on working at the fire even after Mick had become silent. Only when Hugh started asking questions did Vern speak. He growled at Hugh to shut up.

Ev worked up a smoke, offered the sack around, got no takers, and returned it to his pocket. Barnum sat in sulky silence. Finally Vern began apportioning the food into four tin plates that he afterward pushed at each man, the last plate going to Mick, along with a dark look from the range boss.

"Did he act suspicious?" Vern asked quietly.

"No. He said he'd just gotten into the country. He acted friendly, even had a smoke with me."

"Then he doesn't suspect anything yet."

"I'd say he doesn't, Vern."

"Did he say anything at all about what brought him here?"

"No, and I didn't push it any, either. Maybe he isn't a gunfighter, Vern, but he sure as hell looks like one."

"Did he look at all like the girl?"

"Not a bit."

Vern filled his mouth, chewed a moment, then said: "If he didn't, chances are he ain't her brother."

"And he's too young to be her paw."

"Husband," muttered Everett, "or boyfriend."

Hugh started to speak. Vern cut across those forming words with a cold comment: "You should've followed him, Mick."

"Perhaps. The notion came to me."

"Then why didn't you?"

"Several reasons, Vern. But mainly because if he'd caught me at it, he'd have his first inkling that something was wrong up here. He'd have been suspicious."

"We know the country, he don't," Vern said. "We can spy on him from the rimrocks."

Vern finished eating, scrubbed his plate with dirt, sat back on his heels, and ran a slow, penetrating stare up and around the forest fringe encircling the valley. He had made up his mind about something but did not impart whatever this was to the others.

He said: "Hurry up, you fellers. Let's get mounted and back down to the home place. Amos's got to be told."

Hugh watched the range boss get up. "He said for you to stay up here and that he'd relieve you tomorrow, Vern."

The range boss turned, his lips twisted, his eyes black and murky. "That was before Holt Jackson showed up. We'll all be going back together."

Which is what they did after their meal was completed. Vern led on out of Salt Valley in the same position he'd held on the way in. Behind him rode Mick, then Ev, and finally Hugh Barnum, his pink skin reddened from exposure to the day-long sun, his face looking puzzled about something.

Mick, who knew the country round-about, kept watching for fresh tracks leading out of the valley ahead of Vern. He did not find any, which meant that Holt Jackson had either not located this trail, or had deliberately avoided it.

There were other ways down out of the hills. None so easy as this well-traveled pathway, but to any trail-wise rider who had no wish to encounter others, it would not be difficult to get out upon the southward plains. All he had to do was study the skyline, locate a notch in the hills, and set his course in that direction. Every notch was a cutbank cañon, and each cañon debouched upon land lower down. That was the way Nature worked; springtime run-offs for a million years had cut those cañons. Any rider worth his salt knew that.

Where the four of them left the forest, coming on to the undulating, open country foothills below, night was fast falling. With it came one of those little evening winds that moaned through trees and ran on, low across the grasslands. Usually, coming over snow fields higher up, these little blows were cold. This one was no exception. Up ahead, Vern took loose his sheep-pelt coat, shrugged into it, and behind him each of the others did the same.

They came within sight of Rafter M with the help of that diminishing moon. The land over which they passed was a sheet of ancient burnished copper, old and as seemingly indifferent as the moon itself, which made that soft light.

There was an orange, square glow over at the main house when the four of them swung off in front of the barn. Vern tossed Mick his reins, saying: "Put him up for me. I'll go tell Amos."

For a long time they had been quite silent. Now Hugh said: "Maybe Jackson wasn't alone."

Ev and Mick turned to look at the smaller man. Hugh went on the defensive at once. He'd been getting rough treatment this day and being defensive came easily now.

"Well, you don't know he was alone, do you, Mick? You said you seen him standing in there among the trees, but you never said you seen his horse. Maybe he had friends back in the trees where his horse was."

"I got the impression he was alone, Hugh. He said he'd come over the peaks into Salt Valley. He didn't say *we* came over the peaks."

"Maybe he wouldn't say that anyway, though."

They all heard the door over at Amos's place open and close. Everett stirred. "Come on, let's put the horses up and go make some coffee."

They trooped on into the barn, offsaddled,

cared for the animals, then trooped on out again, bound for their log bunkhouse. They had the lamp lit and the coffee pot on when Vern and old Amos came shoving in out of the chilly night. Amos ranged over them all with his bleak stare, but addressed Mick Gleason when he spoke.

"Vern's been telling me about your meeting with this stranger . . . this man who called himself Holt Jackson."

This was a statement, not a question, so Mick stood over by the stove listening and saying nothing. There would be more, he could tell that by old Amos's expression, and whatever it was would not be pleasant. Mick could also see that. His insides knotted up. He was beginning to think he knew what Vern had looked so grim about up at the line shack, and what old Amos was eventually going to say now.

As Amos spoke, Vern shrugged out of his riding coat, passed over to the foot of his bunk, and hung the thing from a peg over there. Ev did what he always did when he felt a little less than sure of himself; he began making a cigarette. Hugh and Mick, over by the crackling stove, simply stood and looked at Amos and listened.

"I got the same misgivings about this Holt Jackson you boys also got," said old Amos, his shaggy white hair still pressed down from the hat he was no longer wearing. "And I figure we got to make danged certain he finds nothing, that he keeps on going south looking for his friends. But if he don't . . ." Amos paused, looked around to get and hold their full attention. "But if he don't, boys, if he gets a bee in his bonnet, then we got to protect ourselves."

That was exactly what Mick had thought old Amos was going to lead up to. It was the only plausible alternative. Up at the line shack Vern had recognized this before he or Ev or Hugh Barnum had even thought this far ahead.

"Now then," went on Amos. "Tomorrow we're going hunting for this Jackson feller. We're going to spy on him until he makes his decision to ride on or to stay, whichever he does. But we're also going to make damned sure he's alone, because if he ain't, we also got to know that, too."

"If he is alone," said Mick through stiff lips, "and if he finds something that'll make him stay . . . what then?"

Amos's look over at Mick was unmistakably ruthless. "Every one of you in this room knows the answer to that as well as I do. We kill him."

The coffee began to boil. For a short while this was the loudest, in fact the only, sound in the bunkhouse. Vern Howten quietly walked across from his bunk, adjusted the stove-pipe damper, took down five battered tin cups, and placed them side by side. He did not at once pour the coffee but he stood listening to its atrophying sounds, as though waiting until the grounds settled was at that moment the only really important thing in life.

Ev smoked his quirly until it burned his fingers, then threw it into the ash box beside the stove, stood up to get his cup of java, and sit back down again at the one permanent piece of furniture in all cow ranch bunkhouses, the big, long table.

Mick and Hugh also took their cups to that table. When Vern came over, he fetched along the fifth cup for Amos. The silence was awkward and long-drawn.

"There's no other way I know of," said Amos ultimately. "It's us or him . . . providing he doesn't ride on. Sure as God made green apples he's one of 'em."

Hugh Barnum spoke up, sounding puzzled. "I got the feeling you fellers know something I don't know. I mean . . . what the hell . . . we done what was plumb right. We caught a band of moonlighters red-handed, and we fixed their lousy wagon for 'em. There's no cowman within a thousand miles who wouldn't say we done just exactly right. No lawman, either, for that matter. But you fellers keep acting like you got to defend yourselves, like we committed some awful crime. Now I don't see it that way a-tall and I know for a fact won't any other . . ."

"You made your point," growled old Amos. "You don't have to repeat it all, Hugh."

Amos looked at the others. They looked back at

him. Amos raised his bushy brows at Vern. The range boss shrugged morosely, looking into his coffee cup. "Go ahead and tell him," he mumbled. "I guess now it's come to the point where don't any of us have the right to hold out on the others."

"Tell me what?" demanded Hugh, puckering his forehead.

Amos ignored Barnum. He looked at Mick and Ev in the same silently inquiring way. They both nodded back. "Vern's right," assented Mick. "He's in it up to his ears, too. If anything happens, he's got a right to know what to expect."

"Hugh," said Amos heavily, swiveling his bitter old eyes to the smallest man among them. "You recollect that little scrawny one we jerked up first, down there when we hanged them two?"

"Sure I remember. Littler'n I am."

"Hugh, that one was a girl."

Barnum's eyes jumped wide open, stayed that way for a moment, then turned shrewd, turned sly and knowing. He smiled. "You fellers can't fool me," he said stoutly. "You boys can't kid me. I ain't that dumb."

Chapter Eight

The following morning they left Rafter M's yard in an easy lope, heading southward. Amos had the right idea; it wouldn't be necessary to track Holt Jackson. It wouldn't even be necessary to find him. All they had to do was get up in the rimrocks and wait, as they'd done before, because if Jackson came riding down onto the grasslands, he'd be visible at once, and it was that grasslands country where the secret graves were, that was important, not Holt Jackson.

Hugh Barnum had recovered from his shock of the night before, but he was still having difficulty believing that little one had been a girl. Once, before they started up into the rocky lands, he got over beside Ev and said: "I thought Vern said something about a she or a her at the line shack yesterday, but I figured I'd heard wrong."

"You didn't hear wrong," muttered Ev, pushing his animal to get ahead of Hugh. "Mick and Vern and I saw her. It was a girl without any doubt."

"I don't understand, though," Hugh said, shaking his head.

Ev was ahead now. He twisted to say: "You don't have to understand. None of us do. She's done-for and can't hurt nobody . . . it's this Jackson feller we got to sweat about now."

Old Amos, as grim and unkempt and taciturn as ever, was the first to reach the rimrock edge. He obviously expected a long siege up here because he got down, tied his horse, loosened the *cincha*, took down a bundle from behind the cantle, and walked out to the edge of smooth stone, there to sit down, cross-legged, like an Indian without once looking back to see what the others would do.

They followed Amos's example, sat out there loosely close, for now, indifferently watchful, letting the first sun rays come along pleasantly to warm them in their coats. Old Amos unwrapped his bundle after a while, handed the cold meat to Vern Howten, and wiped grease off a pair of binoculars. With these he made one sweep of the immense expanse of grasslands below, adjusted the eyepieces, then put the binoculars aside to say: "You fellers did a good job at the graves. I could pick up your wagon trail but that was about all."

Mick looked at the older man's back, thinking that from up here things would look a heap different than they'd look to a rider, if one should appear and trace out those wagon tracks. The only real way to conceal graves was to let one winter's snow and frost obliterate all marks.

He'd thought that when they'd been dragging brush over those graves. What he thought now was that they weren't to get that respite.

Ev made a smoke after a while. The sun's good

springtime warmth burned against their backs and sides. A little band of horses came plodding around that westerly shoulder of solid granite to where tall grass grew, slowed there, and began peacefully to graze. Dead ahead and much higher, that eternal snow field glinted soft pink, its towering spire naked rock all the way down to timberline, but after that, where ranks of stiff-topped pines stood, the mountain chain south-ward looked bristly and darkly shadowed.

Vern, squatting there with his coat collar turned up, his lean, swarthy face and jet-black eyes expressionless, watching, looked for all the world like an Indian. He hadn't spoken a word since they'd left the ranch.

Hugh would have spoken, but, sitting as he was in layers of total, gloomy silence among the others, had a dampening effect upon him. He squirmed a little from time to time, reached under himself once to brush away annoying pebbles, but he did not break the hush.

The sun glided higher, its heat increased, and by 10:00 those watchers shed their coats. By 11:00 Ev was so drowsy he got up and went back to check the horses. Vern and old Amos sat on as flinty-faced and lethally patient as only deadly men could be.

With the sun almost overhead Amos finally moved. He lifted his binoculars, slowly set them against his face, and remained motionless for a long time. As he lowered the glasses, held them out to Vern, he said: "South and west. Far below the granite shoulder but coming on from around it."

Everett, long since returned from his walk, looked at Mick. Those two exchanged a knowing glance. Hugh, sitting by Ev, cross-legged, leaned far forward straining to sight movement out where the sunlight burned brightest.

Vern lowered the glasses to his lap and sat completely still for a long time, staring south-westerly with slitted eyes. Hugh, beside himself with curiosity, looked from the binoculars in Vern's lap upward to the range boss' face. He wanted in the worst way to ask for the glasses but Vern's expression held him silent.

Amos growled: "Let Mick look. He knows him by sight."

Mick accepted the binoculars, set them to his eyes, and made a slow circuit until he saw the horseman. He wasn't certain, although the rider was a powerfully compact man as Jackson had been, until he spotted that red-rusty hair when the stranger removed his hat, swiped at sweat upon his forehead, and replaced the hat.

He handed the glasses back to Vern. "That's him. He's got kind of chestnut-colored hair with red to it. That's him all right."

Hugh eased back, looking alert and interested. "Now what?" he asked.

"We wait," replied Amos shortly, and they waited some more, sat there with their crossed legs getting numb and their eyes beginning to ache from the straining after a while, but never once looking away from the distant horseman who seemed to be moving with exasperating slowness from west to east.

They all knew, long before they saw Jackson pause down there, that he would cut across the wagon tracks. When he stopped, they sat there, tense and expectant. If he kept on riding east, they could sigh in relief. If he didn't do that, if he swung to follow those tracks . . .

He did neither. He got down from the saddle, made a smoke, and stood for a long time looking all around, examining the countryside from north to south, from east to west. He did most of the things a stranger would do in an unfamiliar place. Then he remounted, turned, and rode directly toward their rimrocks with the sun against him, moving leisurely and loosely along the way a man would ride who expects nothing.

Mick felt Everett go loose beside him. Ahead, old Amos's bony shoulder points also dropped. He swept up one work-roughened old hand, made a pass at his mustache, dragging at its corners, then let the hand drop. Amos was obviously as relieved as they all were, yet he did not say anything even yet, which was just as well because Jackson, when he was within a mile of the rimrocks, did a peculiar thing. He straightened in the saddle, lifted his reins, and suddenly spun his horse around and around in a tight little circle.

Amos stiffened, watching this maneuver. Mick heard the breath rush out of him. Vern, too, drew slowly upright, his body going rigid. These two read something into that exhibition of reining. They said nothing to Mick or Everett or Hugh, though, not even after Jackson stopped, sat still a long moment, then casually turned his horse and went slowly pacing back westerly the way he'd come.

"What was that for?" Everett finally asked, speaking to no one in particular. "Unusual place to work your horse on the rein just for the hell of it."

Amos got stiffly upright, stamped circulation back into his legs, and exchanged a glance with Vern. It was clear old Amos was not going to speak. He started past, heading back toward the horses, but Vern stopped him in mid-stride.

"I thought we agreed last night not to keep anything from one another," he said flatly, looking over at Amos.

For a second or two that bleak, leathery old sun-layered face with its contrastingly white longhorn mustache was set hard against the range boss. Then Amos grudgingly nodded. "I reckon that's right enough," he grumbled. "Tell 'em, then."

"Jackson knew we were up here," stated Vern to

the others. "I don't know how he knew . . . maybe he was just guessing, but that little circling maneuver he did down there . . . that's Injun. When Injuns want to signal to their friends to come down where they are, they spin their horses around and around like that. Jackson was doing that on purpose to let us know he knew he was being watched. Sort of sarcastic-like, I'd guess."

Hugh Barnum shuffled his feet in the silence. He looked around, then said to Vern: "How could he know we were up here? For that matter how could he know anything? He told Mick he just arrived up here yesterday."

Amos shot an annoyed look at Barnum. "I ain't concerned with when he came into the country, confound it, and you shouldn't be, either, if you got a lick of sense. What we got to worry about is whatever made him sure someone'd be watching him today."

Vern and Amos suddenly swiveled their cold glances over to Mick. They seemed suddenly to have become suspicious. Mick read those expressions right and slowly, adamantly shook his head.

"I told you everything that was said between us, word for word. He had no reason to suspect a thing, as far as I'm concerned."

Ev, coming to his pardner's aid, said: "Seems to me without firing a damned shot, this Holt Jackson's got us all spooking at shadows and looking sideward at one another. Vern, you said yourself maybe Jackson was just guessing we were up here."

Barnum began bobbing his head up and down in agreement with these words but the others totally ignored him.

Finally Amos dropped his eyes, pursed his lips, and reluctantly said: "You could be right, Ev. I'll tell you, boys, let's get on home and do a little figuring on the way." Amos raised his head slowly, looked at every one of the others separately, made no move along toward the horses, and concluded quietly: "Last night we talked about what would have to be done if Jackson got suspicious. Let's think on that while we ride back."

Amos and Vern rode side-by-side, desultorily speaking back and forth once the five of them were back down out of the rimrocks. Hugh Barnum rode up behind those two, looking glum and uncomfortable, while back a hundred feet or so behind Hugh rode Everett Tarr and Mick Gleason. It was getting along toward midafternoon, the far-away hills had a kind of smokiness over them, and heat was rising up from the springtime earth in a way that ordinarily would have produced a drowsiness, only now it didn't.

"It puzzles hell out of me how he could've known we were watching him," said Mick. "Unless he found something yesterday or today that'd make him suspicious about Rafter M."

But Ev had been doing some tall thinking since they'd descended from the rim and now he said: "Listen, Mick, if he found the sign of his friends, that's all he'd need to be suspicious. Look at it like this. Suppose he knew they were coming up to hit Rafter M's horse herd again. Suppose he knew that, and trailed 'em up onto our range . . . then, poof . . . they upped and plumb disappeared. What would he think? For that matter, in his boots, what would you and me think? We'd figure, since Rafter M owned all the country hereabouts, that Rafter M knew something. We'd have to figure that. What else is there to think? Them rustlers didn't get the horses . . . all he had to do was look around this morning as he rode around our range to see that we still got one hell of a lot of horses . . . but his friends are gone like they'd been swallowed up by the earth."

Mick, riding along with his head down, his brow furrowed, and his lips sucked flat with concentration, ran all this through his mind before saying: "If you're right, Ev, then he'd also figure we'd be somewhere up high, watching him this morning."

"Yeah."

"Go a little further with it, Ev. If you were in his boots, what would you think now?"

"I already did that, and I come up with the idea

all over again, Mick, that the smartest thing for you and me to do is roll our blankets and get to hell out of this country as fast as two good horses can take us."

"You think he'll find the graves, don't you?"

"I wasn't thinking that at all. I was thinking we shouldn't hang around to find out whether he finds 'em or not."

Mick grimaced. "Makes a feller feel mean and dirty, though, running out."

"You got to be alive to feel mean and dirty, Mick. You said yourself he looked like a gun-fighter."

Mick blew out a big breath, held forth his right hand, and said: "Give me some of your tobacco, will you? A mess like this makes me want to take a stiff drink or a smoke."

They entered Rafter M's yard with a lowering sun hanging above a westward peak, red as blood and as large as life. They put up their horses in long silence, then Amos accompanied them across to the bunkhouse, entered beside Vern Howten, removed his hat, and flung it down upon the table, followed it down, and said: "What's the verdict?"

Vern crossed to the stove, peered into the coffee pot, found enough residue there from morning, and set the pot squarely over the hot plate. He afterward very methodically began to build a fire. All this without looking around or speaking.

Hugh Barnum went to his bunk and sank down,

clearly unwilling to be the first to answer Amos's question.

"Mick?" said the old cowman. "Everett? What you fellers think we got to do?"

Ev scowled and shook his head. Mick tossed his coat upon a bunk and kept his back to Amos. He had nothing to say, either.

From over by the stove Vern straightened up, swung from the waist to gaze at the others, and said very quietly: "Kill him. Find his camp, sock him away like we done the others, and forget it."

Chapter Nine

"We split up," said old Amos the next morning at the bunkhouse after breakfast. "We split up and take our carbines. My personal guess is that he's south and west of the ranch in the trees some-where. He'll need water for his camp and that's where the best campsites are."

"Or north," submitted Vern Howten. "He knows about Salt Valley and the northward mountains. No man, fearing trouble, goes poking around new country if he can help it."

"All right," assented old Amos. "Vern, you ride the Salt Valley country. Hugh, you and me'll take the southward sweep. Mick, you and Everett go down to the grasslands, split up, and comb the easterly countryside. Agreeable?"

No one said whether it was agreeable or not, but they all hiked along behind old Amos to the corrals, snaked out their saddle stock, rigged out, and left the Rafter M yard, heading in their respective directions.

Long before Mick and Ev split up down on the plain, Ev said: "Listen, Mick, we can't keep putting this off. We got to make up our minds whether to stay, or cut and run."

"Tonight," said Mick. "Tonight, after the others are bedded down, we'll roll our hoops. That suit you?"

"Last night would've suited me better," grumbled Everett, squinting southward where wagon tracks were visible. "But all right. We'll cut loose tonight." Ev brought his glance back. "You going to sashay down and look at the graves?"

"Yeah."

"I'll ride north to the rims and parallel 'em for a while, but I don't think either of us'll find any tracks or any camp."

"I don't, either. He'll feel familiar with the southwest or northwest country."

"Mick?"

"Yeah?"

"You figure to shoot him?"

Mick reined up, puckered his brows at Ev, and said: "I don't rightly know, for sure. If he makes a play, I'll probably try. How about you?"

"I been wrestling with that ever since last night.

I sure don't want to shoot him. There's been enough killing over that abortive horse raid."

"Yeah. Well, this afternoon I'll head back the same way we came down here. See you then."

Mick booted his beast out into a slow lope southward. He held the beast to it for a mile, then slackened off, permitting the horse to use its own judgment about following the wagon marks.

He came to the first grave site, paused only long enough to see that nothing had been disturbed, and that there were no new horse tracks there, then pushed along to the second grave site.

The land was still and hushed. Mick looked in all directions and saw nothing, not even the little split-off band of grazing horses they had all seen the day before. The sun, as before, was pleasantly warm, visibility was so good he could see a bare patch in that far-away upland snow field, and just as he came near the second spot, he scented cattle. Everything, so far as he could determine, was exactly as it should be.

He didn't stop at the second grave site, but rode slowly on down toward that land swell where the three of them had so pleasantly conversed two days before. There were no fresh tracks down there, either. The only thing at the third spot that held his attention was that rope-burned cotton-wood limb overhead. He winced at the sight of those brownish bruises in the pale bark.

Where Hugh Barnum had made the lariats

fast at the trunk, there were unmistakable dark stains in the growing soft bark, too. Mick worried about these telltale marks; he tried telling himself that unless someone knew about lynchings, he probably would miss the significance here. But it was no good. In the first place this Holt Jackson was not that simple. In the second place, what else could have made those bruises except a rope? Finally, this far from any place, why would men lash their lariats to a tree? Not to hold some roped critter; there were two rope stains. Any pair of riders who'd perhaps roped a cow or a horse wouldn't attempt to snub it. They'd simply ride off in opposite directions, stretching out the beast between them.

This, of course, left only the obvious alternative to explain those rope marks. Mick stood a while in the shade of the cottonwood with his dismal thoughts, then mounted up and turned northward again, heading back toward the rimrocks and the adjacent broken country where he'd take the homeward trail and probably run into Everett.

He was half across that dreary expanse of open country when a soundless kind of abrupt vibration rode the overhead air. There was no sound, really, only a kind of reverberation, so faint as to be hardly noticed, yet in his present frame of mind noticeable enough to jerk him straight up in his saddle, looking westward and holding back a pent-up breath.

There was no repetition, however, of that tag end of an echo, if in fact that's what the minor disturbance had been. His horse scarcely flicked its ears as it paced along, the stillness bore down as strongly as before, and the sun, sinking westward again, was turning the rimrocks, the forested slopes, even the plain itself, into an afternoon shade of soft saffron.

Mick told himself it was the naked feeling, being out here alone where he could be easily watched from those same lifts and rises from which he and the others had also watched another man that made his nerves edgy. Also, it was the great depth of silence, and perhaps the reason he was down here, all conspiring to make him overly sensitive. He brushed the tenseness aside and made steadily for the northward trail that led back to Rafter M. In fact, shortly before he got into the murky afternoon shade near there, he told himself that the others had probably come up with as little as he had. Maybe, for that matter, Holt Jackson had even left the country.

He was grateful for the protection of the trees northward of the rimrocks and halted among them, ostensibly to give his horse a blow, although, since he'd gone on around the rimrocks and hadn't climbed them, the animal couldn't have been tired. He wished for a smoke, but since he very rarely carried the makings with him, this was a futile wish, so he just stood there, gazing somberly back downcountry. Ev, he was sure, would still be east of him. He was athwart the homeward trail and no new tracks were visible heading for home, so he stood and waited and thought.

His primary consideration, as the afternoon wore along, was about leaving Rafter M. He couldn't make himself feel the least bit heroic about this running out on McCarthy and Howten and even Hugh Barnum after having had a hand in the same grisly business. Yet he kept recalling Ev's rock-like logic, and how Ev had been correct right along. If they didn't leave Rafter M, there was an excellent chance they might remain there through eternity, now that this big stranger was in the country, obviously seeking those six dead men and that one dead girl whose last initial was the same as Jackson's last initial.

It left a sour taste in a man's mouth and a bitterness in his gut, thinking of running or staying. Either way a man couldn't look at himself in a shaving mirror and feel like patting himself on the back.

An approaching horseman put Mick's thoughts to scattered flight. He took his own beast into the trees, stepped up over leather, and waited, his heart solidly beating.

It was Ev. He came rocking along, looking with his head slightly swinging from side to side. Evidently Ev wasn't feeling altogether easy in his mind, either. Mick kneed out to meet him.

Ev stopped, let Mick come alongside, reached up to shove his hat back, and said dully: "Another day like this and one cup of black coffee, and I'll be ready to claw my way up them northward peaks, getting out of this country without any help at all."

Mick grinned. "See anything?" he asked. "You look nervous as a cat at kitten time."

"No, I didn't see anything, and if you want a thrill, just go riding through all them damned shadowy places, wondering when a big red-headed feller's going to jump out and throw down on you."

Ev shook out his reins, eased back as his horse resumed its homeward way, and shook his head morosely. He didn't even bother to ask Mick if there'd been anything suspicious out on the prairie, but Mick told him anyway. He also told him of those rope bruises turning noticeably brown on the hang tree. Finally he asked if Ev had felt or heard anything that seemed sort of like the far-away shock waves in the air of a dynamite explosion.

Ev hadn't felt anything like that. "Maybe distant thunder," he offered. "Or a landslide somewhere back in the mountains under a peak somewhere."

"Yeah, maybe," agreed Mick, liking the idea that's what the peculiar sensation might have been. "I wonder if the old man or Vern had any luck?"

"To tell you the honest to God truth, I hope they don't, Mick."

"Yeah?"

"I'd be willing to forget my war bag and bedroll tonight, if we might awaken the others slipping out with 'em, and just hightail it. How about you?"

"No, sir," returned Mick stonily. "I ain't that scairt, and besides I got sixty-seven dollars sewed into the border of my Hudson Bay blanket that it took me three years to save, and that I'm not about to relinquish just because Holt Jackson's in the danged hills."

Ev subsided. As they rode along homeward, his spirits revived until, within sight of the ranch yard, he was able to say dryly, making a pertinent joke: "Looks like everyone got home ahead of us. I wonder if that's because they don't any of 'em care much about getting caught out in the trees after dark?"

Mick said nothing in response to this. He was looking ahead where two figures, one lank, raw-boned, and attired in a threadbare old blanket coat, and the second man, just as leaned down but not quite so tall, were shuffling around three horses.

Dusk was descending, though, and for the final half mile the details of those onward figures were blurred by it. Ev ran a glance around the Rafter M buildings, set so they were in a rough circle that put a man in mind of forted-up Conestoga wagons.

"I liked it up in here," he murmured. "Never seems to get too hot, like down in the Utah country. Nor too cold, like up in Montana around Cross Timbers."

Mick still said nothing,

"Sort of pretty country, too, and livestock do real good. . . ."

"Shut up, Ev."

Tarr's slouching-along frame drew up stiffly, his head swung. "What d'you mean, shut up? What's eating you?"

"Look yonder down there in the yard. What are Amos and Vern doing?"

"Why, offsaddling . . . what else?"

"Like hell they are," murmured Mick. "That's no saddle they just took off the third horse and laid out there."

Ev whipped around, activated in this by the abrupt, brittle tone of his pardner's voice. He let his horse carry him along almost to the yard's most eastern edge where the brace of them passed between an unused smokehouse and a wood-shed, before he lost any of his stiffness. By then it was plain enough to both him and Mick Gleason what old Amos and Vern Howten were doing—they were unloading a corpse.

Amos turned from the waist to watch Mick and Ev come forward. He remained like a statue until those two younger men hauled up and sat there, staring down where Vern was placing a canvas over the wide, open-eyed countenance of Hugh Barnum.

"Dead," rumbled old Amos. "Shot clean through and dead as a stone."

Mick looped one split rein, stepped down with the other one in his hand, and bent slightly to see that waxen face, that little circlet of red froth on Barnum's shirt front.

"Yeah," he muttered in a near whisper. "I wondered if it wasn't a far-off gunshot. It was maybe two, three hours ago. It wasn't an echo and it wasn't a report . . . just a kind of shock wave traveling in the air."

"That'd be about right," said Amos. "I sent him down toward the plain while I kept along the Salt Valley trail. I guess he'd been gone maybe an hour, maybe a mite less, when I heard what I figured was just one gunshot, only louder, more like a dynamite blast than a gunshot."

Amos tugged a pistol from his waistband, handed it to Mick, and waited until the younger man had opened the gate, seen the expended cartridge in there, and handed the gun back, before going on. "What made it so danged loud . . . they evidently both fired at the same time. Hugh got off his shot . . . you saw that in his gun."

"Yeah."

"And Jackson got off his shot, too." Amos pointed down at that frothy red place in the center of Barnum's shirt. "Jackson was the better shot of the two. That's all there was to it. I spurred down there, but Jackson wasn't no place around. Only Hugh . . . lying there, drilled plumb center."

Vern waited until Ev got down and stepped over, then said: "Give me a hand with him. For tonight we'll put him in the barn."

Ev bent, while over his back the sun dropped away and that sad, lonely in-between time was upon the land again.

Chapter Ten

They buried Hugh Barnum east of Firewood Creek and a quarter mile north of the ranch buildings before sunup the next morning. It didn't take nearly as long to dig his grave as it did those other holes for the simple reason the ground near the creek was crumbly and moist and as black as moldy silt usually is. Then they returned to the bunkhouse, sorted out Hugh's gatherings, looking for the little mementoes drifters sometimes carried in their war bags that would indicate where Barnum was from and who his next of kin were.

"Nothing," pronounced Vern, when everything had been dumped out of the little war bag. "Razor, steel mirror, needles, thread, and bandage wrapping, that's about it. No letters, no writing at all."

Amos, more experienced in these things than

the others, said: "All right. We'll hang his outfit in the barn loft, and the trifling stuff like that razor, the thread and needles, you divide among your-selves." Amos went to the door, passed through, halted, and looked back. "We'll be riding in an hour, boys, and this time we're not to go pussy-footing around after that damned outlaw. This time we're going to hunt him down like he was a bronco buck Indian on a hate trail. Be back after I eat."

Mick and Vern and Everett drank coffee but didn't eat. It made a man's appetite atrophy, seeing all Barnum's pitiful possessions dumped out there on the table. Vern went out, after a while, which left Mick to exchange a look with Ev.

Ev said: "Well, I know what you're thinking so you might as well go ahead and say it."

"What am I thinking?"

"That we didn't leave last night like we planned."

Mick drained his cup, considered the grounds, and shook his head. "Not exactly. We sort of had to hang around and bury Barnum. Makes a feller feel treacherous enough thinking of running out, Ev. But I don't blame you for saying we ought to stick around until Hugh was socked away, when you mentioned it last night."

"Thanks. But, Mick . . . that's done, so how about tonight?"

Mick stepped to the stove, refilling his cup,

held the pot up toward Ev, got a negative head shake, and put the pot aside. "Barnum was a pain in the tail sometimes," he murmured. "But that feller still had no right to kill him. Damned outlaws running roughshod over honest folks don't exactly sit right with me, Ev."

"You said he looked like a gunfighter."

"I know. And he did, too."

"He could pot one of us next, you know. A feller doesn't stand much chance riding among these damned trees, Mick."

"Well, Ev, I'll tell you what. I made up my mind. I'm not saying my decision is right. I guess mostly what I decide isn't right, but you head on out if you want."

Ev looked up from his position at the table. He squinted his eyes. "You mean you're staying?" he asked.

"Yeah."

"Oh."

Ev dropped his gaze to those scattered gatherings upon the table, his expression solemn and his eyes seemed a little understanding and a little grim—and also just a little sad.

"Oh hell," he growled listlessly, after a while. "You're right, Mick. Barnum wasn't much, maybe, but that still don't make it right for some lousy renegade to shoot him for doing what he had every right to do."

"A feller believes in certain things, Ev."

"Yeah. Outlaws riding roughshod over folks is no good. You're right, Mick. We'll stay. At least until this other one is paid back for Barnum."

Mick smiled, sipped his coffee, said: "Better have another cup, Ev. It's likely to be a long time till supper." He looked toward the door as Vern reëntered the bunkhouse.

"Fed the horses and caught the ones we'll be riding today," said the range boss. He started for the stove. "Toted Hugh's outfit up into the loft, too." He filled a tin cup, held it in both hands to warm his fingers, and gazed over where Mick was sitting at the table, his back to the stove. "You fellers got plenty of carbine shells?"

"I expect so," replied Mick without looking around. "How many does it take for just one man?"

"We don't know it's only one man, Mick."

"Vern, if there was more, we'd sure know it by now. Naw, he's alone."

Mick finished, got up to put his cup to soak in their wash bucket, shot Ev a surreptitious glance to see his pardner's expression, then went over and shrugged into his riding coat.

"I'll go commence saddling up," he said, and departed from the bunkhouse.

The uplands were misted over by a shroud-like pale and diaphanous ground fog. It was transparent and lay in wavy layers halfway up the northward mountainsides. It was a clammy thing, but, since it would disappear as soon as the sun arose, Mick paid it no particular heed as he walked to the barn.

Up at the main house there was a weak shaft of lamplight in the rear of the house. Old Amos was having his breakfast. It was a fact that the bizarre business of burying the dead, with some men, was not allowed to interfere with the affairs of the living, such as a hearty breakfast before taking to the saddle in search of a killer. Mick shook his head, stepped into the barn, shot a look around, and wondered how long it had taken old Amos to get that hard and callous—or maybe it was just being sensible. Barnum was dead, and that was a damned fact, and before they got back to Rafter M today, they'd be hungry as bitch wolves for sure, so maybe Amos was just being sensible. He walked into the fragrant gloom, leaned on his saddle, and wagged his head again.

Sensible or not, he couldn't have forced a mouthful down this morning if Old Nick had been prodding him with a six-tined pitchfork. He still had some of that grave-side black soil under his fingernails.

He was making loose his lariat when Ev walked in, saw him, and approached. Ev looked like he'd lost his last friend. He went past, got his rope, too, and when Mick passed on out back to snake out his mount, Ev trudged along mechanically. At the gate he said: "Vern's sitting in there going through Barnum's gatherings again, drinking coffee and looking like he just swallowed a fistful of green worms."

Mick cocked an eye. "You don't look real cheerful yourself. I don't expect any of us do. Before you came into the barn, did you look up at the main house? There's a light in the kitchen. The old man's eating breakfast. I think, if we were smart, we'd borrow a page from his book. Hugh's dead and that's that, so now we hunt down his killer and square the debt . . . and that'll be that, too."

Ev stepped through the gate. The eating horses, wise in the ways of their world, left off and began to mill, to twist in and out, to crowd up in a corner of the log corral. The oldest, most knowledgeable horses dropped their heads so the loops Mick and Ev built would not settle around their necks. It did not always avail, though; both cowboys roped their choice of mounts and led them back into the barn. Vern and old Amos were there, ropes in hand, also set to catch their mounts for the day. They hiked past Mick and Ev side-by-side, bound for the corral, without a word.

Outside, the sun, still down behind an eastward rampart, sent forth its preceding orange-yellow first light, and although this did not dispel the ground fog, it did brighten the upland considerably with a soft, sallow light.

Somewhere southward a cow bawled for her calf. Moments later a quavering answer came back. The sky turned dusty blue and in the hillside pockets shreds of the night lingered, dark and smoky. Mick led his saddled animal outside, took a last tug at the *cincha*, turned the horse once, then stepped up. The horse didn't do anything although he had a little hump in his back.

Ev came next, and later the old man and Vern also led their beasts outside before mounting. Vern's horse gave a few half-hearted crow-hops, more as though he thought it was expected of him than because the saddle blanket was cold on his back. Then old Amos led out.

For a half mile, or until they were well away from the ranch, Amos said nothing, just rocked along in his everlasting old blanket coat for all the world like a gaunt old scarecrow. He reined down eventually, where the broad, well-marked Salt Valley cut-off showed up, pointed with his chin at a twisted, fainter trail leading westward, and said: "We'll start hunting where Hugh got it yesterday, only this time we won't split up. He'll be expecting trouble now, and he'll be watching."

They lined out single file and worked their way in and out of trees and gloomy shadows. Here the ground fog lay like watered milk. Occasionally they came across a place where the sun's warming rays filtered down through overhead pine limbs. These pleasant interludes became more frequent as they passed along, indicating that the sun was fully up now, although they could not, in the heart of the forest, see it.

An hour later the old man left the trail following the punched-down tracks of a ridden horse. A little farther along they encountered another set of prints, only those second ones, from the flung-up earth they'd scattered, had been made by someone in a hurry.

"Mine," explained Amos, knowing his cowboys would be wondering. "I was north of here when I heard the shooting. I came busting down this way and made them marks."

They were close enough to the last fringe of trees when they eventually halted to see the grasslands out beyond. There, sunlight lay over everything like new gold.

Amos got down, stalked forward, squinted earthward, and stood stonily still. At his feet the pine needle matting had been furiously churned. He pointed to a particularly disturbed place and said: "That's where Hugh was lying. Over there's where Jackson must've been."

Mick dismounted, dropped his reins, and stepped carefully ahead, studying the ground. He heard Ev and Vern Howten moving around behind him but paid them no heed. He found where a horse had been tied, estimated that the animal had been at that one spot for several hours, went to the spongy edge of a tiny seepage spring, and bent far over to consider the imprints there.

"It was his camp all right," he mumbled to the others. "Here's where a little pan set . . . probably his fry pan."

No one answered or came over to look. Ev and Vern were tracing out the route Barnum's slayer had used when he broke away after the shooting. They stayed with this track until it struck hard ground out beyond the forest fringe, then turned reluctantly back and joined Amos and Mick.

Ev said: "It's guesswork from here on. As hard as that ground is out yonder, and as many Rafter M horses running around out there, we'd need a hound dog or an Injun to track him down from here."

"He'd go east," rumbled Amos. "East or back north up toward Salt Valley. Them's the only two parts of my range he's familiar with so far."

"We could split up," suggested Ev.

Amos shook his head adamantly at this. "No, by God, we did that yesterday and look what happened. No, we'll start out combing the eastward range, then we'll cut around north by the rimrocks and head for Salt Valley."

"It'll be dark by then," said Vern.

"Then let it get dark," snapped old Amos. "I'm going to tell you boys something. When you're after a man, don't do your hunting in fits and starts 'cause you only favor him that way. Keep after him. Don't let him rest or eat or even stop for a drink of water. I learned that from the Injuns and it works every time, believe me."

Amos went back to the horses, swung up, and eased out. The others also got astride and passed down through the last tier of trees, out onto the sunlit plain, swung east, and plodded along.

Out here the land was empty in all directions, except for one bunch of grazing Rafter M cattle. Out of lifelong habit Amos led them to within viewing distance of those critters, then right on by.

An hour later, when they came around that red stone granite shoulder of land that lay adjacent to the northward rimrocks, Ev began riding a little wide from the others, his head tilted downward, his body forward in the saddle.

"What is it?" called out Amos.

"Shod horse marks."

"You plumb sure?"

Ev looked up, annoyed. "See for yourself," he said brusquely, halted, and pointed downward as the others crowded up around him.

Those tracks were infrequent but by zigzagging they could occasionally pick one up. The ground was hard, the grass thick, and only where little patches of hardpan and the gait of that shod horse happened to coincide were those tracks discernible, because wherever hardpan pushed up through top soil, no grass grew.

"Heading southeast, I'd guess," offered Mick. "He's riding about the same way we saw him ride from the rimrocks that time he run his horse in that little circle."

"That's the direction of the cottonwoods," muttered Vern.

Mick looked swiftly at the range boss. For a second his heart stood still.

"He won't find anything down there, damn him."

"Yes he will," contradicted Mick, and explained about those telltale rope burns.

Amos and Vern put their grave looks upon Mick without speaking for a long time after the younger man had finished speaking. Finally Amos said in a brittle, unmistakable tone: "All right. We got a job to do now, for sure. Let's go get him."

Chapter Eleven

They rode all together in a tight group, loping hard southward. It wasn't as it had been before. Now they had a definite goal and a definite purpose, and this inspired in each of them new life and fresh resolve.

They struck the fading wagon wheel marks, swung along over them, and in this manner passed the first two grave sites. No one said anything but Mick and Ev looked earthward. Then they were past, north of that rolling land swell, beating along through the golden sunlight.

Amos was the first around the land swell, his blanket coat flapping around him as he sped along. The hang tree was in sight now, and standing there at the base of it, shadowed by overhead, leafy limbs, was a burly man and a big, stocking-legged blood bay horse.

The stranger had his back to them, but even if he hadn't, they still would have caught him like that because, until they burst around that land swell, they had been hidden from any onward viewing.

The blood bay horse, though, less intent than his master, gave the warning by flinging up his head. He may have softly snorted, too, but Mick, who was watching the stranger, could not determine this. All he was sure of was that the stranger suddenly whipped around, saw those four riders rushing at him, every one of them armed with carbine and belt gun, and threw himself toward his horse.

Amos yanked back, jerked his Winchester out, threw it up, and fired. It was a wild, frantic shot and missed by yards. Then Amos's horse did what he should've done back at the barn and not this late in the morning; he ducked his head when that Winchester blew the silence apart and bucked high and hard, forcing the old man to drop his carbine and concentrate on riding the storm out to avoid being set afoot this far from home. He bucked and bawled and swapped ends heading straight for Vern, who had to battle his own animal to keep it from panicking, too.

Mick didn't bother with his carbine. Neither did Ev. They had a killer in view and went after him, driving in as fast as they could. They were not quite in pistol range when the stranger spun out westerly in a dead run.

Mick spurred furiously but the distance kept widening. Ev, off on Mick's right, suddenly leaned, jerked loose his Winchester, slid off his horse, and stepped down. Momentum catapulted him forward another fifty feet before he could slow enough to drop to one knee and raise the carbine.

The stranger, riding twisted in his saddle, threw three rapid rearward pistol shots at his pursuers. The range was too great for handguns, but those blasting explosions were sufficient to cause Ev to wince as he got off his first shot. It went wide. Ev levered the carbine, raised it, and fired again. This one was much closer, close enough in fact to force the stranger to flinch, drop low, and rowel his horse unmercifully. He raced westward in a belly-down run. By the time Ev was ready to fire again the blood bay horse was a hundred yards beyond range.

Ev got up, eased down the hammer of his gun, and turned to look for Mick, who came walking up beside him, leading his animal. Mick was breathing hard.

A quarter mile back Amos was visibly stiff with rage on his ridden-out horse. He and Vern came loping forward side-by-side. Before they got close, Ev said: "If he'd been riding a Rafter M horse, I'd have nailed him sure."

"Damned thoroughbred," growled Mick, looking past where the escaping man was growing small upon the grassy plain. "Either that or a race-horse, dog-gone him."

"Was it Jackson, Mick?"

"Yeah, it was him all right," Mick answered bleakly. "And I'll tell you something else, too. He knows what happened over by those cotton-woods."

Amos and Vern stopped ten feet away and did not dismount. "Do any good?" the old man asked flintily, his face still pale with anger.

Ev shook his head. "The second shot was close but not close enough."

"Then come on," snapped the old man. "We're a long way from being through with him yet."

As Mick was swinging up, Amos asked him the identical question Ev had asked. Mick gave the same answer: "Yeah, it was Jackson."

They loped for an hour with that small, distant figure still in sight. Ev reloaded, letting his horse follow the others. When he was finished, he unlooped the reins, got up beside Mick, and the pair of them cantered along without speaking.

When the sun was nearly overhead, Amos

slackened off. They were still well in sight of Jackson, but a mile beyond gun range. Amos began to swear, not at Jackson but at the horse under him that had chosen the one moment to break in two when he shouldn't have. He didn't bust the animal over the head with his hard-twist, coiled lariat as most cowboys would have done, but he swore without a pause for two full minutes and never once repeated himself, which awed the men with him and also kept the animal under him on edge for the blow that never came.

Jackson did not swing northward as they expected him to, flee into the forest, and lose himself there. For some reason that intrigued his pursuers and baffled them as well, he remained out in the open country where they could stay after him without any difficulty.

It was nearly 2:00 p.m. by the descending sun before Mick thought he knew what Jackson was doing. It was driven home to Mick when the horse under him began to lag, to stumble, and to breathe like a locomotive.

"No use keeping this up!" he yelled ahead to Amos. "He's doing this on purpose. That horse of his can outrun these critters hands down."

Mick slowed to rest his animal. Ev also slowed. Vern Howten ran on another half mile, then, when his mount stumbled from exhaustion, Vern also slowed.

Amos was the last one to admit they'd been

outrun and he did not give in with very good grace. He cursed his horse some more as he dragged him down to a lumbering walk, letting the others come even with him.

"He's tough," pronounced Mick, speaking of the distant rider, "and he's got the kind of sense of humor that likes to make fellers feel almighty inferior. Like signaling us on the rimrocks that he knew we were up there. And like now . . . leading us on for the fun of it to show us he's got the best horse under him."

"He'll laugh out the other side of his damned face before I'm through with him," swore old Amos, shaking with fury, his mahogany face so pale with gorge it came close to matching his mane and mustache for paleness. "I'm going to kill that man if it's the last thing I ever do!"

Vern said nothing. Neither did Ev Tarr. They slumped along, watching that distant horseman with the sun now in their faces, occupied with their own unvoiced thoughts.

"He's got down, out there," said Mick.

They all strained to see that this was true. Jackson was walking along on foot beside his animal, evidently cooling the beast out and giving him a moment's relief from carrying Jackson's weight. Amos, as pale in the face as death, glared ahead for a while, then roughly gave an order.

"Mick, you and Ev cut north here. You won't be able to get around him. He's too *coyote* for that, but try and get up even with him against the trees so's if he tries to swing northward into the forest, you can cut him off."

Mick jerked his head at Everett. The pair of them pushed their tired animals over into a slow, easy canter, and broke away from old Amos and Vern Howten. When they were a mile out, Mick said: "It's a waste of time and it's unnecessarily hard on these horses. He'll know what we're up to."

Ev agreed, but he also said: "I'd rather do this, though, than ride along with old Amos right now. He's fit to be tied."

They were almost to the northward trees when Mick, looking back, saw Vern and Amos boot their animals over into a jolting trot. Far westward, Jackson was back in his saddle again. He obviously had guessed the purpose of Mick and Ev and was at last beginning to angle northward toward the forest's protection.

"Too much of a lead," said Mick emphatically. "Damned if I'll kill this horse just to get within rifle range, either."

Ev approved of this, so while they kept along toward a westerly juncture with the place where Jackson would get into the forest, Vern and old Amos tried running Jackson down again from the rear.

The failure of Amos's men was complete a half hour later when Jackson halted just short of his first tree shadows, spun his horse in that familiar little round-about circle, mockingly telling his pursuers to come along, then rode out of sight where forest gloom lay thick and silent and ageless, all around.

Amos and Vern reached that place first where Jackson had faded out. They waited with impatience until Mick and Ev came up.

"I told you to go after him," snarled old Amos, his anger of before still smoky in his glare. "You could've been closer, damn it all."

"But never close enough," stated Mick, "to get a shot, so we decided not to kill these horses trying."

Amos purpled but before he could speak, Vern Howten said something that made hard sense to them all. "Out in the open he doesn't have to know the country. All he needs is two good eyes. But up in here we got the advantage. He can't use the speed his horse's got, and he don't know the mountains like we do. Amos, you going to lead out, or shall I?"

Amos squared around in his saddle, eased out, and rode in through the first ranks of trees. At once it got twenty degrees cooler. It also turned cathedral-like with a great hush that permeated everything. For an hour they rode along with Amos hunched forward, following fresh, shod horse tracks. At length he halted, sat a moment in quiet thought, then, without a word, started onward again. He had obviously just run through his mind the sites Jackson might be making for, and just as obviously he had come up with the idea of Salt Valley.

It wasn't the only place there was water, but it was the only nearby place Jackson might know of where there was water *and* grass for his mount.

But a mile farther along those shod horse marks in the spongy mulch swung suddenly eastward, puzzling Vern, Mick, and Ev as much as this seemed to perplex old Amos. Eastward and southerly lay Rafter M. Farther on easterly was only more forest until a rider struck the rimrock country.

Vern said: "He did that to throw us off, Amos. I'll bet he's circling around and heading for Salt Valley still."

"Maybe," muttered the older man, plainly confused. "Maybe so, Vern." Amos twisted to look back. "We shouldn't split up, though," he said, indicating that he was now confronted with two choices—staying on Jackson's tracks as they were doing, or trying slyly to outmaneuver the hunted man by sending someone on to Salt Valley to anticipate the fugitive. "Damn it all, anyway."

The others sat stonily awaiting their employer's decision. It was a long time coming, and when Amos spoke again, his pronouncement was a surprise to all of them.

"We'll figure you might be right, Vern. We'll *all* ride to the valley."

They had to backtrack nearly a mile, swing upcountry as far as the marked trail leading to the salting grounds, then pass along this with the reddening sun flashing into their faces intermittently through forest shadows, before they came out upon the upper lip of Salt Valley's drop-off.

"Now we'll split up," stated Amos. "Mick, you take Ev and ride plumb on around the valley to the north. Vern and I'll sashay on around southerly. We'll all meet at the line shack. Stay out of sight in the trees now. If he's around here, we got to see him before he sees us. If you spy him . . . shoot. Don't give him no warning . . . just shoot."

Mick and Ev went threading their way around the upper reaches of Salt Valley with lengthening shadows turning solid, turning steadily more formless and continuing, as they made the encircling ride. There were no established trails up where they rode, only an occasional deer path leading usually downward toward that emerald clearing and its water hole below.

Once, where they had to seek a way around a giant windfall pine, they halted to have a smoke, and here Ev asked if Mick didn't think, perhaps, that Jackson might now head on out of the country. "Man, I would if anyone'd taken after me like we done after him . . . four to one and hell-bent on doing a killing."

"It would depend on the man," replied Mick thoughtfully, exhaling and watching the smoke.

"The man and the reasons he had for running or not running. Jackson's got reason not to run now, Ev. He saw those rope burns on that cottonwood tree down there. He knows for sure what's been going on up here. If he had doubts before, he sure hasn't got 'em now. Nope, I've got him sized up as not the running kind at all. And I'll tell you something else, too. I don't like riding around in these dog-goned trees with him knowing for sure now what we did to his friends . . . his wife, too, maybe."

Ev agreed with the last part of this. He followed Mick on around the windfall and kept his head swinging from right to left and back again. "Old Amos's off his head," he eventually said, as they began descending toward the lower country. "He must've been hell on wheels when he was thirty years younger if the way he's acting now is any indication. He's going to kill Jackson or die trying."

Chapter Twelve

It was late in the day when the four of them came together again down at the line shack. Amos was sullen from failure, but Mick and Ev were hungry more than anything else. They, and Vern, went about rustling up a meal while Amos walked far out and around, looking for sign that Holt Jackson had camped in the valley. He found none, so when he returned, squatted down to eat, he told the others that Jackson must have another hide-out, which was now obvious but which the others did not confirm or deny as they ate.

"It'll be somewhere around the ranch," said old Amos. "He's probably been watching the place."

"Well," opined Mick, "if he was just watching out of curiosity before, after seeing those rope burns on the hang tree, he won't be as curious hereafter as he'll be likely to wait for a good pot shot at one of us."

"All of us, you mean," muttered Ev.

"More reason to keep on hunting him," said Amos. "I'll do a little slipping around tonight after we get back, but I want him to see the lot of us ride into the yard first. After he's satisfied we're all home, and it gets plumb dark, I'll sneak out."

"Where'll you look?" asked Vern. "There's a heap of country to be covered. He won't be hiding in the obvious places."

"Sure he won't, but I'll have all night to find him. I've done my share of moccasin work, don't forget that. I've slipped up on Dakotas. Slipping up on white men is plumb easy after you've stalked a few dozen Injuns."

They left Salt Valley with the sun teetering atop a blood-red westerly peak, rode slowly but carefully up into the forest, hit the homeward trail, and kept on it without another stop until, with the sun quite gone, they came down to broken, foothill country again. Rafter M's buildings were gloomily visible in the thickening dusk.

Amos led them on to the barn where they off-saddled without a light, turned their horses out, forked hay over the corral fence, then trooped together in plain sight of any watcher, over to the bunkhouse.

It was murkily dark by this time. The northward hills loomed starkly against a sooty sky. Mick had an uncomfortable sensation as he stepped along as though eyes were boring into his back somewhere out there where the formless night was settling. Amos was at his side, slumped of shoulder and grimly thoughtful. Ahead was Vern Howten. In front of the range boss Ev was the first one up the bunkhouse steps. Mick saw his dark shape suddenly falter, saw Ev throw out both arms for balance, then stumble, and go down with a curse.

The others got up onto that small porch and halted as Ev got back upright, brushed himself off, and bent to peer downward.

"Who left this damned thing right where a man'd fall over it?" Ev demanded. He seemed about to say something else, but he didn't say it. Instead, he straightened up slightly, mumbled something, reached out to push the bunkhouse door open, then grabbed whatever it was he'd stumbled over and lugged it on inside.

Mick lit the table lamp while Amos and Vern, silent and puzzled, stood back, frowning. Light fell across a badly punished saddle. There was dirt on the thing, and pine needles, too. There were deep scratches on the swells where a horse had rolled with the rig on him.

For a while no one said anything, then Vern let off an audible sigh, stepped closer, stared hard, and stepped back. Mick looked swiftly at the range boss. Vern's normally ruddy face was pale.

"Whose is it?" Mick asked.

"His," murmured Vern, staring at the saddle where Ev had dumped it on the big table. "That feller we hung with the girl. It was his."

Amos's face twisted with disbelief. "How do you know that?" he demanded.

Vern stepped in close once more. He pointed to the right side of the rig, to the right jockey, the right rosadero, the right side of skirt where dark, stiff stains were visible, darker by far than the other leather.

"I shot him as he was coming at me. I told you fellers that."

"What of it?" old McCarthy demanded.

"I shot him in the right hip, Amos, that's the what of it!"

Mick went around, fingered that stained leather, found it more pliable than the rest of the rig, wiped his hand unconsciously upon his trouser leg, and looked across at Amos and Vern.

"It's old blood," he said. "See for yourselves."

"I don't have to see," mumbled Vern. He turned, crossed to the wood stove, and began puttering around over there with the coffee pot and the fire-box, his back to the saddle and to his companions.

"It's beginning to make sense now," Ev said, speaking quietly. "Jackson had this thing. Maybe he found it yesterday or the day before on that dead feller's horse. He had it hid between the ranch and Salt Valley. Today, when we run him, he led us toward Salt Valley on purpose. While we were scouting around for him in the valley, he got this thing from wherever he had it hid, rode down here bold as brass because he knew we were a long ways off, and left it on the bunk-house porch, knowing damned well we'd fall over it."

Amos was totally silent as he moved up closer to finger that limp leather. He afterward bent far over, placed his hand close to the lamp, and stared at it. Without a word he, too, straightened back and wiped his hand along one trouser leg.

From over by the stove Vern said: "Blood?"

Old Amos nodded his head up and down.

"He's got guts, anyway," Mick reluctantly conceded.

"That ain't all he's got," Amos finally said, his tone bitter. "He's got nearly all his answers." He turned away from the saddle, looked at each man in turn, said: "He's got to die and damned quick now." Then he passed over to Vern at the stove. "We can't let him get out of the country to fetch back the law."

"We didn't aim to let him do that, anyway," growled Mick, who dropped down at the table, eased back his hat, and began to push out of his riding coat.

"Yeah," retorted old Amos. "But now he just might try it. No man in his right mind's going to stay around where four other men are set on killing him. I think, until today, he maybe didn't know how all of us felt. But he sure as hell knows now, and he also knows why."

Ev, who had never before spoken up to Amos, now did. "Listen!" he exclaimed. "That feller's not going to run. I don't give a damn what you think, Amos, this Holt Jackson's not the running kind. Do you have to get hit in the head with it before it soaks in? We're not the only ones who got good reason to want a man dead. Jackson's maybe got even better reasons . . . seven of 'em."

Vern, seeing the brittleness that came up now between Ev and old McCarthy, spoke ahead of anything more either of them could say.

"The coffee's hot, get your cups," he said, turning toward the stove. "What we're talking about is water under the bridge. He's out there. He's set to kill any or all of us if he can, and that's that."

"No that ain't that," snapped the old man. "We're not going to be no sitting ducks for him. We're going to get him first."

"Sure," said Vern, sounding tired now. "Here, have a cup of java."

They sat and sipped and were quiet for a long time. Where flickering lamplight fell across their faces, they looked wicked and solemn under that meager light. Upon the table the dead man's scratched and torn saddle loomed large until Mick, with a grunt, got up, removed the thing, and dumped it over in a gloomy corner where they wouldn't have to see it. As he was resuming his seat, he said: "A feller thinks of a dozen things looking for another way out, only nothing'll work. You can't buy a man off when he's got the reasons Jackson's got. You can't even scare him off with big odds."

"Scare him off," snorted Amos. "We don't want to scare him off. We got to keep him from talking . . . ever."

Vern got up, refilled his cup, sat down again, and cradled the cup in both his hands. His expression was haunted. After a while he got up again. This time he went to his bunk, dug among his blankets, and came up with a pony of whiskey. He poured a generous amount into his cup, then wordlessly passed the whiskey around, pouring the same stiff jolt into Ev's cup, into Mick's cup, and finally he halted by Amos.

"No thanks," McCarthy said gruffly. "I got work to do tonight yet." He looked up. "Save it for morning when I get back. With a little luck we'll have something to celebrate."

The atmosphere got stale after they'd been sitting a while longer, so Mick arose, put his emptied cup aside, and began removing his lashed-down holster and shell belt with the obvious intention of retiring.

The others sat watching him for a while, then Ev also began to remove his weapon belt. He bent over by his wall bunk, hung his hat carelessly from a wooden peg, hung his gun belt over the hat, sat down, and kicked off his boots.

Amos arose finally, put his cup on the table, and stalked over to the door. With his hand on the latch he said: "Vern, put your hat over that damned light until I get out of here." Vern complied and Amos disappeared out into the moonless, black night.

Vern slowly removed his hat, slowly turned, and looked at Ev. "It gives me the creeps," he murmured.

"What does?" asked Mick.

"Thinking of him slipping around out there in the blackness." Vern crossed to his bunk, dropped down, and resumed speaking. "I know him. You boys don't. He'll shed his boots, put on those old moccasins he's got over at the main house, take his carbine and a big old knife he's

124

got, and slip out the back way into the trees. I'll tell you fellers something. Amos is in a lot of ways more Indian than white. If he finds Jackson, he'll use the knife if he can. He's done it before. When I first went to work here, there were still a few old Indian bucks around. I've had 'em tell me some of the things he's done. It's enough to make a man's hair stand on end."

Vern arose, unbuttoned his shirt, yanked it off, and sat back down to get out of his boots. To do this he simply grasped the shanks of each spur and pulled. The boots came off, he dropped them, stared at them a moment, then said: "This time he's got more reason to bury that damned knife in a man's kidneys than he ever had before, too. Those other times it was only stolen horses or a butchered steer maybe. This time . . . well . . . he could lose the whole blessed shooting match, ranch, cattle, and all, if it ever got out he hung a young girl."

Mick worked his way down under his blankets, propped his head on one arm, and said: "Don't go underestimating Jackson, Vern. He's ridden rings around us, and now he'll be about as easy to catch hold of as a greased pig."

But Vern wouldn't be convinced Holt Jackson had a chance against old Amos. He wagged his head back and forth, sitting on the edge of his bunk. "I told you, Mick, you fellers don't know

125

Amos. He knows more tricks about stalking a man than you can shake a stick at."

Mick shrugged, swung his gaze over where Everett was also getting down under his blankets, said—"Well, I sort of hope he makes it."—and dropped down upon the pillow he'd fashioned from his riding coat.

"Sort of," said Vern sharply, beginning to scowl. "You better more than just sort of hope he makes it, Mick, because you're in this up to your ears, too, you know."

"How can I forget it?"

"Supposing he doesn't find Jackson?" asked Ev. "Supposing Jackson's hightailed it? He could do that, you know. He left us that danged saddle so's we'd know he knows. Maybe now he's decided to go after help."

"Aw," growled Vern, "a little while ago you almost took old Amos's head off saying Jackson wasn't the running kind. Make up your mind, will you, Ev?"

"All right," Ev shot right back. "Then let's suppose something else, Vern. Let's suppose Jackson gets Amos instead of the other way around. Then what, Vern? Then what do we do?"

"You're talking like a fool," growled the range boss. "There's about as much chance of that happening as there is of building a snowman in hell."

Ev wasn't so sure of that. He said: "Every time we've come onto Jackson, he's made monkeys out of us. What's more, he acts like a feller who's no novice at this hide-and-seek business. And that horse he rides is the fastest critter I ever saw."

"I didn't say he wasn't a top hand outlaw, Ev. What I said was that he can't hold a candle to old Amos at what's going on out there tonight . . . not on old Amos's own ground."

"Aw, shut up you two," growled Mick from deep in his blankets. "If you got to argue about something, argue about which one of you's going to climb back out of your sougans and blow that cussed lamp out."

Ev and Vern raised up, looked at the table. In their preoccupation neither had remembered that the last man to bed was obliged to kill the light. Vern swore mildly and kicked back his blankets. As he was moving forward toward the lamp, Mick spoke again.

"And while you're up," he muttered, "bar the door, too. All this talk of folks slipping around in the dark with scalping knives . . . well . . . just bar the damned door, will you?"

Chapter Thirteen

Mick rolled out when it was still dark, washed, shaved, dressed, and went out to feed the horses. He kept his eyes moving even after he was inside the barn, passing through toward the pole corrals out back. He didn't really expect to encounter Holt Jackson, but he didn't intend to be caught off-guard, either.

After he'd done the chores, he went back to the bunkhouse. Ev and Vern were getting up and one of them had lit the lamp.

"See anything?" Ev asked.

Mick shook his head, went to the stove, and poked up some coals, threw more wood into the firebox, and straightened up to yawn prodigiously.

"Amos isn't up yet," he said. "No lights at the main house."

"Probably didn't get in until late," muttered Vern, buckling on his shell belt. "I'll go see what luck he had while you fellers rustle breakfast."

After Vern left, Ev filled the wash basin with cold water, plunged his hands in, and swore. "Someday I'm going to work at a cow outfit where they got hot water to shave with," he grumbled, "and when that day comes, I'll never leave."

Mick worked at making gruel and coffee. He was still doing this when Vern returned, looking perplexed. As both Mick and Ev turned, Vern said: "He ain't over there. The danged house is plumb empty."

A quick chill passed down Mick's spine. He recalled all the assuring things Vern had said the night before, but could not now find a single substantiating line in the range boss' expression.

Evidently Ev couldn't, either, for he said to Vern: "Eat up, then let's go looking for him."

They did that, but none of them ate very much. Instead, they were all occupied with where to look. Vern had the answer to that. "I know the round-about country best, so I'll lead out and you fellers stay with me." Vern left his mush untouched and his coffee cup half full. Ev did better; he finished his entire breakfast, but where he ordinarily would have gotten seconds, now he didn't. He simply crushed on his hat, walked over to peer out, make certain it was still dark enough for them to leave unseen, looked back, and said—"Come on, it'll be light in a little while."—and stepped outside.

The yard was still, shadows lay thick, and the only sound came from around where Mick had forked feed to the saddle stock.

Vern walked across to the main house, passed around this weathered old building to the rear, pointed to the nearest spit of trees, and moved forward without saying anything.

They were as quiet as unseen twigs underfoot permitted as they began their encircling stalk. Off in the murky east a thin rind of faintness firmed up. From time to time as Mick swung to appraise that brightness, it seemed to broaden. By the time they were parallel with the barn, the corrals, and the bunkhouse, northward, a steely kind of dismal light lay in a soft flush over the upland world. This helped visibility; it also helped them become targets if Jackson was still around waiting for targets.

Vern knew how the land lay very well; he avoided every site where an ambusher might be lying. He also investigated every boulder field, every tree clump, and every patchwork clearing where Amos undoubtedly would have also looked. He cut back, farther northward, and by sunup the three of them had covered more than a mile without actually having really covered more than a third of that distance with their trailing and back trailing.

Finally, just before that far-away red ball sprang up over earth's far curving, Vern motioned them up close, halted, and said in a very low voice: "He ain't up here or we'd have found him by now. We'll head on around to the west and keep up this skirmishing back and forth until we cover every lousy foot of ground hereabouts."

"Hell," grumbled Ev dourly. "How do we know Amos didn't go five miles out in his stalking?"

"We don't," snapped the range boss. "And if we got to, we'll keep up this combing until we've gone five miles out, too. But we're going to find him . . . or them . . . or something."

They found something right after the sun popped up, flooding the land with its rushing golden waves of light. Mick was on Vern's right uphill a hundred or so yards, when he came upon it. A carbine lying unfired atop a matting of needles two feet thick. It could have been thrown there, dropped there, or abandoned there, but in any of those circumstances it was hard for Mick to reconcile himself to its being left behind voluntarily. He hissed downhill at Vern, at Ev, flagged them northward with his arm. Before they reached him, Mick picked up the weapon, eased back the slide, and peered in. There was a cartridge in the chamber ready to be fired. He was still considering this fact when Vern came up, stopped dead still, and stared.

"That's Amos's gun," said the range boss. "Where did you find it?"

"Right where I'm standing. You can see its imprint there."

Vern took the gun, also examined it, handed it to Ev for another inspection, and slowly twisted from the waist to throw a narrowed look out and around. An increasing brightness burned into the shadowy forest gloom where they stood. It had as yet very little warmth, but its brightness helped Vern.

"There it is," he murmured, twisted half around. "There's the trail I've been looking for. Look yonder, those are boot tracks."

Mick peered around Vern, could determine nothing, walked southward a dozen or so yards, and halted. It was difficult to make out the tracks, except for the indisputable fact that whoever had made them carried considerable weight that drove his boots deep down into the needles, they wouldn't have been noticeable at all.

"It'll be Jackson," stated Mick, "who made these tracks. Amos doesn't weigh enough to sink down that deep."

"And," added Vern, coming up to gaze at the marks, "Amos wasn't wearing boots, either. I'll bet you a month's pay on that."

Ev strolled up, studied the tracks very briefly, turned right, and started carefully and slowly tracing out the route of those marks. When he'd gone a hundred yards, he abruptly halted.

"I'm guessing," he said softly to his companions. "But right here where the soil is all scuffed and roiled, Amos found his man and jumped him. I'd say he probably smelled or heard Jackson back there where his gun was lying, and dropped it there to have both hands free."

Vern stepped gingerly around that churned ground bending here and there to examine particular indentations closely. "It was quite a fight," he mused aloud, then saw something, bent, and put forth a hand, drew it back, and stared at it, saying quickly: "Blood, by golly. There's blood on this little bush over here."

Ev went forward to see that blood but Mick didn't. He eased around those two, stepping lightly in a widening circle. He paused where those same sunken boot tracks went westerly again, stepped over the tracks, and widened his quartering circle still more. Finally he halted, drew fully upright, and softly called down to Vern and Ev. "Here he is, boys. Here's old Amos."

McCarthy lay on his side. He didn't move as the three riders pushed up to gaze at him. His hat was gone, and as Vern Howten had predicted, there were moccasins on his feet instead of boots.

"I don't see how Jackson could've done it," murmured Vern. He said this twice more, his voice vague, his look bewildered.

"A man ages," stated Mick. He dropped down, eased Amos over onto his back, bent over, and jerked back. "He's alive," he said swiftly. "Fellers, old Amos is alive."

Vern's astonishment left him in a rush. Once more he became authoritarian and efficient. "Where's he hurt, Mick . . . where'd Jackson get him?"

The three of them dropped down to inspect Amos more closely. They did not find any injury until Vern, in the act of raising the older man's shaggy white head to shove his coat under it as a pillow, drew back one hand with sticky claret on it.

"Over the head," Vern muttered, looking from his hand to Amos's ashen, still face. "He caught him over the head."

Mick rocked back on his heels, swung for a long, probing look around in all directions, then gazed downward once more. "We've got to get

him out of here," he said. "Ev, you take his legs."
Ev was moving to obey when out of the middle
distance a man's bull-bass voice called forth,
triggering a nearly simultaneous and violent
reaction in all three of them. They sprang away
from Amos, rolling toward whatever shielding
upthrust was nearest. Vern and Mick went for their
six-guns. Ev, still with Amos's Winchester, jerked
the carbine to his right shoulder and cocked it.

"Hey down there!" came that rumbling shout.
"Put down your damned guns and let's . . ."

The unseen man got no further. Ev, guessing
about where that voice was coming from, fired.
At once the voice broke off.

Mick snapped off a booming handgun shot.
Almost at the same time Vern fired. The morning's
bright, rich silence was blown fiercely apart by
the thunder of these guns. Ev levered and fired,
making a pattern with his bullets, first to the right
of where he thought Jackson was, then left, then
he drove a bullet straight between his earlier
shots.

Mick tried raking the ground in a sluicing
manner in the hope that if Jackson was belly down
out there through the trees, he might score a
blind hit. It was Vern Howten who methodically
shot his gun empty, reloaded while the other
two tried for clean hits, then rejoined the fight
and emptied his gun a second time.

When Mick's gun was empty, he ceased firing.

So did Ev. Vern paused, too, because he was also shot out. When that rumbling voice tried to cry out again, Vern balanced his six-gun carefully, made his judgment, and proceeded to empty his gun for the third time in the direction those yells had come from.

After that there were no more outcries from Jackson. As the stillness returned, lengthened, drew out almost unbearably, Ev said softly: "I think we got him."

"Go look," ordered Vern, reloading again. "You go with him, Mick. I'm going to stay here with Amos in case Jackson tries slipping around us."

Ev had to abandon the Winchester and draw his six-gun; he had no carbine cartridges with him. He and Mick advanced with a hundred yards between them. They flitted from tree to tree, pausing often and straining for movement ahead. It was a bad time for both of them until Mick, lower down and near the breaking-off area where forest and grassland met, halted for a long while behind a forest giant, then said quietly and calmly: "Over here, Ev. Come on, it's safe."

Ev stepped forth into plain sight, walked down to Mick, and stopped. Ahead of them was a red splatter over pale needles—blood.

"He's hurt now for sure," opined Mick.

"Yeah, that's obvious," Ev quickly retorted. "But how hard and where is he?"

Mick pointed southward down through the

final tree fringe with his gun barrel. "There go his tracks. But unless I miss my guess by a country mile, the way he's bleeding, he isn't going to go far."

"What do we do . . . go after him, or go back and help Vern get old Amos back to the ranch?"

"Go back," said Mick as he turned and began retracing his steps. "It's like when you shoot a bear, Ev. Let him den up somewhere and bleed for an hour or two. Then you can finish him easy. Go poking your nose in, getting all fidgety and anxious, and he danged well might come out with a roar and rip you wide open."

When they got back, Vern was standing, wide-legged, beside Amos, waiting and frowning. Mick told of the splattered blood; he also told Vern what he thought they should do—take Amos back first, then return and track down Jackson.

Vern agreed with this mutely. He motioned each of them to take a leg. He himself stepped back, gently lifted Amos's limp shoulders, and growled: "Easy with him now."

They made no rest halts. In fact, they didn't stop at all until they had Amos on a bunk back down at Rafter M's log bunkhouse. He had a bad injury on the back of his head. If his hair hadn't been nearly white, all that scarlet might not have looked so bad, but his hair was matted with it and he still had not regained consciousness.

"Here," said Mick, lifting McCarthy's head.

"I'll hold him up, Vern, while you fetch that pony of whiskey you got and pour some of it down him. Ev, set the coffee to boiling. When he finally comes around, he's going to have the granddaddy of all headaches. That damned Jackson must've pulled up a full-grown tree and hit him with it."

"Pistol barrel," stated Ev, critically examining the wound. "And I'm going to tell you something else, Mick. Old Amos isn't going to come around right away if you pour a gallon of rotgut down him. Put your hand back here and feel . . . his skull's cracked."

Vern, in the act of uncorking his bottle, stopped and stared at Ev. "You sure about that?" he demanded.

"Feel it for yourself," replied Ev. "The bone's busted sure as shooting."

Chapter Fourteen

The loss of Amos's leadership dampened the resolve that had heretofore been the primary motivating factor in Rafter M's savage duel with Holt Jackson, but it didn't do any more than that, and, in fact, after the shock had worn off, the three remaining men turned cold, turned relentless.

"Two of us got to go track that feller down,"

said Mick. "One of us has got to stay here with Amos." He looked at Vern for verification of this. The range boss inclined his head. He had gotten some of his whiskey down McCarthy's throat and more of it down his shirt front.

"Ev and I'll go," Mick went on. "I figure Jackson's about done for out there somewhere."

"Maybe," said Ev thoughtfully. "And maybe, needing help like he does now, he'll try slipping in here, too."

Vern, in the act of easing the unconscious Amos McCarthy back down, looked over at Ev with his bleak, black stare. "I hope he tries that. I sure hope he does."

Mick hesitated a little while longer. When Vern started sopping at old Amos's matted hair with a wet rag, Mick jerked his head at Ev. The pair of them left Rafter M's bunkhouse, stepped out into the morning brightness, cut around behind to enter the barn from its back doorway, got their booted carbines, and returned to the rear yard where the corrals and farther out the willows along Firewood Creek gave them cover.

They went at an angle and on foot up along the creek's crooked willow bank, screened this way from sight, and eventually got back up into the trees. They went carefully now, for if Holt Jackson had demonstrated nothing else, he had proved himself an enemy worthy of respect.

They ultimately came to the place where Mick

had found Amos. From here on they split up, Ev going on uphill a hundred or so yards, still in sight but wide enough in his paralleling onward stalk to permit the pair of them to sweep a lot of country with this skirmish-like advance.

As the morning waned, filtered heat came into the shadowy forest. Shafts of cathedral-like light came infrequently to soften the dimness, and where they eventually came upon those sunken boot tracks again, light occasionally glistened off drops of red blood on leaves, on pine needles, on bare hardpan earth and stones.

Near high noon with the sun only a little distance from its meridian, Mick cut upland until he'd joined Ev. They stopped for a rest, a smoke, and a discussion.

"I don't understand how he got this far," complained Ev. "He's leaking blood like a stuck hog."

"He's tough," stated Mick. "And he's smart."

"Smart don't help a feller when he's running out of blood, Mick."

"I know. We'll find him."

"You don't look exactly pleased about that."

Mick squinted at his pardner. "Should I be? You heard Vern tell what a hell of a stalker and fighter Amos was. Well, I wouldn't classify either of us anywhere near that good. Amos got it . . . how about us?"

Ev carefully trimmed ash off his cigarette with

one finger and thought a moment before saying: "I figure the odds are a shade better'n even now, in our favor. There's two of us, Jackson's bad hurt, and . . ."

"And when a feller gets overconfident," interrupted Mick, "he's asking for a split skull like Amos got. Come on, get on your feet and let's finish with this business." While Mick stood up, waiting, he added: "As soon as we get Jackson, I vote that we saddle up and get to hell out of Wyoming. How about it?"

"Tonight even," said Ev emphatically. "I'm with you one hundred percent."

They resumed their tracking until, where a small glade appeared, the blood sign suddenly stopped. Here, they came together again to examine minutely the tracks and found that Jackson had had his horse tied at the edge of this glade. He'd mounted up here and ridden almost due south.

"Fine," said Mick bitterly. "He's a-horseback and we're afoot."

"One of us could go back to the ranch and fetch some saddle stock."

"The hell with it," growled Mick in disgust. "We'd lose too much time. Let's just keep a-going until we either find him or have to quit when it gets dark."

Another half hour onward they made another discovery. Jackson was making for Salt Valley but he was not using the regular trail. As soon as Mick was certain of this, he grasped his Winchester at the center for easy balance, motioned to Ev, and broke over into a shambling trot.

The pair of them covered two miles like this, and would have made even better time except that the land began to lift in a steady, long-spreading rise that terminated at the slight heights over-looking the valley. Still, they hastened when they could, and with the sun dropping off in the hazy west, they came together in a tree fringe upon Salt Valley's eastern rim. Below there was no sign of Jackson or his horse, but, to experienced eyes the evidence was plain enough that he had arrived here. The cattle down there were steadily gazing toward the line shack. Cattle did not all look in the same direction, keeping close watch like that, unless something quite foreign to them had just passed by.

"Making something to eat at the shack," opined Ev.

"Maybe. And maybe he's taking time out to plug that hole in him, too. Probably got his horse around back."

Ev rolled his brows together in speculation. "We ought to get that danged cussed horse first, Mick. Chouse the critter out of the corral and set Jackson afoot."

Mick didn't reply. He simply hoisted his

carbine, passed along southward as far as the main trail downward, and utilized its easy access until, near the bottom where grass flats took over and trees gave away, he swung on around, keeping, as an Indian would have done, well back beyond the open country.

They made it without incident to a position behind the line shack where they could see the pole corrals. Those yonder cattle were no longer concerned with whatever had earlier captured their attention. In fact, as far as Mick could see, Salt Valley was exactly as it had been the first time he'd ever seen it—because there was no horse in the line shack corral.

"Damn it," he growled bitterly. "He isn't down there."

Mick would have plunged boldly forward out of their shielding shadows but Ev quickly caught him, yanked him back hard, and said very softly: "No? Well, if he ain't, then that line shack's haunted because I just seen a shadow move past the side window down there."

"You sure of that?"

Ev, looking wry, said: "I know a real fine way to find out. Just step out into plain sight and holler."

"Then where's his horse?"

"How would I know? Right now all I care about is fixing him so's he'll be unable to get back to it, wherever the danged thing is."

Mick stood a while considering how to cross

out of the trees, get over the quite open grassland, and come up on the line shack from the rear. There was one advantage; there were windows—square openings without glass—on both sides and in front, but not in the rear wall.

"It'll be a long chance," he muttered to Ev. "But I think, if we're almighty careful, we might be able to get up there. We've got to be awful quiet, though."

"The tall grass'll help," corroborated Ev, but he sounded a lot less than enthusiastic. "If worse comes to worst, we can lie down in it and hide. I'd feel a heap better, though, if there were some trees or rocks out there. I got a feeling Jackson's as good with his Winchester as he is with his racehorse. I keep remembering old Amos."

Mick did not hear all of this. He was wondering just how badly injured the fugitive was. He finally decided that no matter how resourceful and powerful Jackson was, he had to be weak. Taking courage from this, Mick went down to the very last tier of trees, checked his carbine, and stepped forth into plain sight. Ev, back a short distance, held his breath. Nothing happened. Mick started forward with swift strides. He had a long hundred yards to cross and for the first fifty he was almost certain to be safe. The ground here was spongy from years of rotting grass, free of rocks, and, except for the whisper of tall grass striking his legs, yielded to his passage without any obstacles at all.

Ev came forth and hurried to catch up, but he did not walk with Mick. Instead, Ev angled off to one side so that, if they were discovered and fired upon, one shot might hit, but it would also warn the survivor in plenty of time for him to drop down in the grass.

And that is almost what happened, too, except that when they were discovered, Jackson bellowed at them from a side window before he fired.

"Hold it!" he roared at Ev and Mick. "Hold it a minute you two! I've got something to . . ."

Mick dropped from sight in the tall grass like stone, rolled frantically, and fired. Ev, farther out and with a somewhat better sighting on that side window, fired first and dropped down later. It was Ev's bullet, striking with a meaty sound into punky logs that brought Jackson's return fire whipping low through the grass.

Mick got off another round, this time with better aim. He afterward rolled over and over, getting clear of the place he'd fired from, and also trying to reach Ev.

Jackson's next slug came from the rear wall of the line shack where he'd evidently knocked out some chinking to push his gun barrel through. He systematically levered and fired, moving his sights a little to the east each time. He was no novice. Mick had already suspected this, but now he knew it for a fact because those spaced shots were coming steadily on toward him from his right. Jackson had the range down very well.

Mick risked a shout to Ev. "Back!" he called, and changed his own course to roll southward back toward the protective forest again. "Back, Ev!"

Jackson's fire did not slacken nor hasten. He poured that systematic fusillade into the tall grass, and when his Winchester was levered dry, he switched to using a six-gun.

By the time Mick was safely behind those rearward trees again, Ev was also there. Both of them were covered with foxtails and medusa heads, those little clinging, crawling banes of the grasslands. They turned wordlessly and grimly to ridding themselves of the worst of these little sticky annoyances and said nothing until this had been accomplished. Then Mick called Holt Jackson a number of fierce and sizzling epithets before he said: "He's got eyes in the back of his lousy head. Now what? We'll never be able to get up there again."

"He can shoot, too," muttered Ev. "Just like I figured. That talk about the odds being in our favor . . ."

"Never mind all that now, Ev."

"Well, the only thing I know to do now, since we don't stand the chance of a snowball in hell of getting him out of there, is to find his cussed horse and set him afoot up in here. It's a lead-pipe cinch, hurt like he is, once we get him set afoot all we got to do is track him down and finish him."

Mick gave his pardner a pained look and, leaning his Winchester against a tree, resumed yanking foxtails out of his shirt, but he said nothing at all, although it was plain in his face that this alternative did not appeal to him. He had been routed like a ten-year old child, forced to roll all the way back to the forest, and what he now wanted was Holt Jackson's hide, not his cussed horse.

Still, Ev's suggestion seemed the only plausible alternative to stepping out there again and getting downed by lead.

"We'll split up and go around the valley on both sides. He'll have hid his critter some-where back in the trees. But all the time you're slipping around up in here, Ev, keep one eye on that line shack. We can't let him get out of there."

Ev nodded dourly, hooked his carbine in one arm, and turned to go stalking easterly on around Salt Valley toward the main trail. He was privately convinced, since they'd entered the valley from that general direction and had encountered no tied horse, that Jackson's animal had to be on around the westerly curving, where Mick was striking out.

It never once occurred to either of them that the

fugitive, who had outwitted them at every turn thus far, might also outwit them this time, too.

Mick kept his attention divided as he went searchingly along. He not only wished to keep the line shack in sight and seek Jackson's horse, but he also wanted to have some idea where Everett was. It was this constantly ranging watchfulness of his that brought him ultimately to a startled halt when he was some half a mile northward.

Back there, in plain sight before the line shack, was the fugitive. He was sitting atop his horse with a naked Winchester balanced over his thighs, the sunlight showing bitterly from that steel barrel, and Jackson appeared to be watching with considerable interest the progress Ev was making on the valley's westerly rim.

Mick was like stone. It hit him with the sledge-hammer solidness of a physical blow that Jackson hadn't hidden his horse in the forest at all. He'd had the cussed thing inside the line shack with him!

Across the valley a faint, keening cry rang out. Mick turned only fleetingly to see Everett step forth. Ev had also seen that mounted man, sitting quietly there out of gun range of either of them.

Mick switched his stare instantly back. He was just in time to see the fugitive making that little tight, derisive circle with his horse again, before he jogged slowly southward out of sight.

Chapter Fifteen

It was close to 11:00 p.m., dark as pitch and gustily cold from a hustling little wind coming straight off an upland snow field somewhere, before Mick and Ev got back to Rafter M's bunkhouse.

Vern had the stove going, coffee on, and a pot of venison stew simmering. He'd cleaned old Amos up but otherwise McCarthy looked the same. He was pale and wan and utterly limp on his bunk near the door. Flickering lamplight falling across him made it seem that Amos was dead instead of faintly alive.

"What luck?" asked Vern as soon as Ev and Mick stumbled in out of the night.

"None," growled Mick, making for the stove, the coffee, and a bowl of that deer meat stew. "We tracked him to the Salt Valley line shack, tried to slip up on him, and he run us off. Vern, Jackson's more devil than man. I don't care what you figure, he's already thought of it."

"He wasn't hit, then?"

"He was hit all right," stated Ev, warming himself at the stove. "He lost a lot of blood, too. But if that's supposed to weaken folks, I reckon he's never heard that it does, because he didn't sit down and die like a respectable feller would've done. He rode off pretty as you please."

"Which way?"

Mick, warmed by his first cup of coffee, turned and said sharply: "What difference does it make? He won't keep riding the same direction."

"It makes a lot of difference. We'll go after him in the morning on horseback and we'll want to have some idea of which way he's heading because, weak or not, he won't ride all night long, he'll bed down."

"I wouldn't bet a red cent on what that man'll do," Mick muttered, filling a bowl and taking it over to the table where he dropped down tiredly and began to eat. "I wouldn't even bet he's human."

Ev, slower to fill his bowl, less disgruntled than his pardner, said: "How's Amos making it?"

Vern sighed, looked at McCarthy, then away again. "I don't know. Setting legs and arms is no great chore, but a cracked skull . . . that's plumb out of my field. What Amos needs is a doctor, and the closest one's down at Lodgepole, fifty-five miles from here."

"Would he stand the trip?"

Vern lifted his shoulders and let them fall. "Dunno. Amos's pretty long in the tooth. Age counts against a man when he's bad hurt."

"Well," demanded Mick sharply, "he's going to die lying here anyway, so what can we lose by trying to get him to help?"

"I'll tell you what we can lose," answered Vern

149

Howten waspishly, his expression hardening against Mick and his tone turning knife-edged. "We can lose the feller who done this to him. The same feller who killed Hugh Barnum, and I know old Amos this well . . . he'd never forgive us if we didn't get Jackson first, then try to get him down to help at Lodgepole."

Mick resumed eating and turned pensive. Vern's angry retort didn't make much sense to him. What injured man wanted to risk death solely for revenge? None that he'd ever run across. They instead wanted to get patched up so they could have another crack at their foe. He had old Amos sized up as iron hard all right, but not ridiculously so. But Vern, well, Vern was proving himself somewhat different than Mick had up to now considered him. Vern was showing himself more wolf than man.

Ev shuffled to the table, dropped down, and began eating. For a while, until those two had thawed the chill from their bones and had worked out the pleats in their bellies, nothing more was said.

Afterward, with that whimpering wind scrabbling along the outside eaves, they did what they could for Amos, which wasn't much, only wrapping him in blankets against the nighttime cold, and afterward discussed their war against Holt Jackson until Vern finally came up with an idea.

"I could ride over to the Beaver place and get one of their riders to go for the doctor down at Lodgepole," he said, then sat there, watching the faces of Mick and Ev. "I'd just say Amos had an accident . . . fell or something, got bucked off a horse maybe, and lit on his head. They'd send one of their men, and I could be back here before dawn. How's that sound?"

It sounded all right. In fact, as Mick said, it was just about the only alternative to sitting around and watching old Amos slowly die. "If he doesn't come around pretty soon, he'll just plain starve to death. We can't just pour whiskey into him. He's got to have food. Damn it all, I'd give a lot to know how Jackson beat him to it."

"We'll find that out soon enough," said Vern, arising to stride over, take down his riding coat, and shrug into it. "Come dawn, the three of us'll go after Mister Jackson on horseback."

"Wait a minute," interjected Ev as Vern strode for the bunkhouse door. "If those folks over at the Beaver place get too blessed curious, they might ride over here. If they do that . . . if they get to nosing around . . . they might just stumble onto what happened to those rustlers . . . and that girl."

"Leave all that to me," retorted the range boss. "I've known the Beaver Ranch folks for enough years to keep 'em away. Besides, it's getting close to spring roundup time. I doubt if they'll need much encouragement to stay around their own part of the country and do their own work."

Vern opened the door a crack, peered out, closed it, and motioned to Mick, who was closest, to put his hat over the lamp so Vern wouldn't be limned when he slipped out. Mick complied, waited until Vern had closed the door after himself, removed his hat, and shook his head morosely.

"One man out there," he said, "just one lousy man . . . and he's got all of us so buffaloed we're scairt to even step out of our own bunkhouse for fear of being bushwhacked."

Ev went over, refilled his cup, brought the coffee pot back to the table, sat down again, and said: "It only takes one man to shoot you, Mick. I don't see much wrong with being leery of this particular man anyway. What's bothering me now is . . . why are we staying here? Vern's gone. We'll likely never have a better chance than right now for getting out."

Mick, some other time, would have become indignant about this remark; now he did not. "This damned affair's become a kind of personal thing with me, Ev. Jackson's made a fool of me for the last time."

Ev, gazing over the rim of his cup at old Amos, lowered the cup and said softly: "Yeah, you're right of course, Mick."

That whimpering wind rose a little, rattled some loose shakes on the roof, and echoed in the stovepipe. This added to the gloominess that came to permeate the room where those two sat, and if those sounds, at least, broke the otherwise hush, they did not do it in a manner that was less gloomy.

Mick eventually strolled over to have a look at Amos. He got a shock for the old man's eyes were wide open and rationally upon him.

"Amos?" he called diffidently. "You hear me all right, Amos?"

A lull came in the outside wind long enough for Mick, and Ev, too, still over at the table, to hear McCarthy's answer to this.

"I hear you. I don't see you worth a damn but I hear you. Who is it, Vern?"

"It's Mick. Vern's gone for help. I'm here with you, so is Ev."

"Vern's . . . gone?"

"Only over to the Beaver outfit to send for a doctor down at Lodgepole."

"Beaver . . . mustn't . . . know."

"They won't. We talked that over before Vern left."

"Where'd you . . . boys . . . bury Jackson?"

"We haven't nailed him yet, Amos, but we will. How do you feel?"

"Can't move one side of me, Mick. Can't even lift . . . my arm."

"The doc'll likely be able to fix that when he gets here," said Mick, feeling decidedly uncertain about the truth of this. "Amos, how did he get you?"

"Trick," said the older man, his voice beginning to fade out. "Tricked me. . . . It wasn't him."

Ev, hearing that voice fade, left the table to walk over closer. He looked quickly at Mick at those last words, then bent over the bunk to say: "There's two of 'em . . . is that what you're saying?"

"No," came the faint answer. "Just Jackson. But he . . . wasn't there. He was back a ways, waiting."

"How?" demanded Ev, bending lower and turning insistent. "How did he trick you?"

"It was his coat, his hat, half hidden in the dark. He'd stuffed 'em with needles to give 'em body. He . . ."

Amos made a soft, bubbly sigh and lapsed into unconsciousness, his eyes half closing. He went loose all over and seemed scarcely to be breathing. After Ev made certain he was still alive, he straightened around toward Mick.

"Well," he said strongly but matter-of-factly, "chalk up another one for Holt Jackson . . . damn him."

Mick tucked the blankets closer around old Amos's bony shoulders, stepped back, and went over for more coffee. He had his back to Everett when he said: "That feller's had every trick pulled on him, Ev. That Jackson's an old wolf. It wouldn't surprise me a bit if he was to spy Vern riding out and catch him, too." He turned around and leaned upon the table, his stare solemn and unwavering. "And if he's done that . . . if he's gotten Vern, too . . . then I say we got only one thing left to do. Get to hell out of here, make for Lodgepole as fast as we can, and fetch back the law and a posse."

Ev's brow rolled up into corrugated lines. He stood over by Amos's bunk with his unpleasant thoughts for a long while before he replied. "We das'n't, Mick. You know cussed well, if the law takes Jackson alive, he'll tell about that girl getting strangled to death by us."

"We'll have to try and make sure the law doesn't take him alive then. But I'll tell you this much, Ev, we can't do it by ourselves. We've tried when there was five of us. We kept on trying when there was four of us. Now . . . there's maybe only you and me."

"You can't write Vern off yet, Mick."

"No," retorted Mick thinly. "No, we can't write him off until around sunup. But after that we can and we'll have to. And like it or not, Ev, we've got to run for help like a couple of scairt pups. That, or wait around for Jackson to pick us off, too."

"Or," said Everett slowly, very reluctantly, "saddle up and just point our noses west and keep on riding until we see the ocean, Mick." Ev slumped, ranged his weary eyes around the room, halted them over at the table, and muttered: "Any coffee left?"

Mick poured a cup full and shoved it to the table's edge where Ev came up and lifted it. "I've drunk enough of this lousy stuff to float away the last week," he said dispiritedly. "It didn't taste good to begin with and now it's like acid in my guts."

"It's not all the coffee, Ev."

"Mick, we'd have heard a shot, wouldn't we?"

"You're forgetting something, Ev. We never found that scalping knife Vern said Amos had with him. We found where Jackson'd bled and we found Amos's unfired Winchester . . . but we never found that cussed knife."

Ev made a face and pushed the coffee cup away from him. He turned, put his grave eyes upon old Amos in the shadowy corner, deliberately walked over, stripped back the blankets, and peered downward. Mick watched Ev do this. He also watched Ev cover the unconscious man again, and afterward turn, and cross the room to his abandoned coffee cup.

"See anything?" Mick asked.

"Yeah. An empty knife holster on his belt. Where'd Vern put that whiskey bottle of his?"

"Be a bad way to get it, wouldn't it? Someone jump out of the night and sink a foot of cold steel into your back."

"Where'd he put that damned whiskey?"

"Look in his war bag. Ev?"

"Yeah?"

"If he's not back come sunup, we head for Lodgepole. Right?"

Ev didn't answer; he instead went over to rummage in Vern Howten's possibles bag until he'd found the pony of whiskey. He held it out to the light. There was barely enough liquor left for two shots. Walking back to the table, he said: "Want yours straight or in some coffee?"

Straight." They lifted their cups, threw off the last of Vern's liquor in one gulp, put the cups down, and looked straight across the table at one another.

"Like I said," murmured Ev, "we could just saddle up and ride on. No one'd ever know, and after we got clear of these uplands even Jackson couldn't get at us."

"What about him?" asked Mick, gazing over at Amos's fallen-in, gray face. "If Vern didn't come back, he'd lie right there until he died. It might take a week or ten days, but he'd die."

Ev removed his hat, flung it down, and ran a set of bent fingers through his awry hair. "Mick, how'd we get into this? I'm no murderer. I didn't want to kill that girl."

Chapter Sixteen

It was 4:00 in the morning when Vern Howten returned. Mick and Ev hadn't gone to bed, at least neither of them had gotten undressed and climbed down into their blankets, but both of them were stretched out on their bunks and the lamp was still gustily burning.

Mick, balancing on the edge of sleep, heard the horse walk into the yard, heard it come steadily down toward the bunkhouse instead of turning in at the barn as it normally would have done. He sat up, listening. Across the way Ev was sitting up, with his gun in hand, looking at the door.

Vern stepped up onto the yonder porch, lifted the latch, and stopped. He was under two cocked guns. Mick spoke first. He eased off the hammer of his weapon, holstered the thing, and said: "How'd it go?"

Vern came on in, shed his coat, and went over to rattle the coffee pot. "All right. They sent a rider down to Lodgepole. I told 'em Amos got bucked off in the rocks on his head."

Ev got up off his bunk, mightily stretched and mightily yawned. "The pot's empty," he informed Vern.

"So I see," muttered Howten, and went to work making a fresh pot. "How's Amos?"

"He came around for a few minutes about an hour after you left last night," replied Ev. "Said Jackson tricked him by filling his clothes with leaves, and when Amos jumped what he thought was Jackson, he was waiting back there and knocked him out with a gun barrel . . . or something like that."

"That's close enough," agreed Mick. Then he said: "Vern, you see anything on the ride over or back?"

"Going over . . . no. Coming back . . . yes." Vern finished with the coffee pot, placed it carefully on the hot plate, and turned. His features in the smoky yellow light looked slack and whiskery and gray. "I never saw nor heard a blessed thing going over and I kept a sharp watch, too. But coming back I saw where someone on horseback had trailed me."

"Going over they trailed you?"

"Yeah. One man." Vern let that lie there a moment, then wagged his head. "I never heard a blessed thing, and except for a little wind it was quiet as a graveyard most of the way to the Beaver Ranch." He paused again to look significantly at the other two. "That's a ride of seven miles one way, fourteen miles round trip. I never heard a blessed thing."

Ev wagged his head over that. It was eerie, in his view, that a man could track another man for seven miles without making a sound or arousing the other man's suspicion, particularly when Vern had been as alert as Ev thought he'd been. "Like a damned ghost," he muttered.

Mick agreed with this but he was thinking of something else. "Why wouldn't he make a run on you, Vern? What kept him from getting you from behind with that damned knife he took off old Amos?"

"I don't know. That's what bothered me after I found those blamed tracks. I'm telling you that last five miles back here were mighty uncomfortable. I kept expecting it and yet it never came." Vern looked straight over at Mick. "You want to know what it's like to walk five miles on foot beside your horse, expecting every second to have someone knife you or shoot you from behind a tree in the damned night . . . try that ride over to Beaver and back sometime."

Mick let this go by. He was interested in why Jackson had not tried to get Vern. "Maybe," he speculated slowly, "he's too weak from loss of blood. Maybe he figured that if he didn't down you with the first slash or stab, you'd be too much for him."

"Maybe a lot of things," growled Vern, walking over to stand beside Amos's bunk, staring bitterly down. "I don't think he's so weak, Mick. He rode seven miles trailing me. A weak man couldn't do that. I think he was probably behind me all the way back, too, but I don't know about that. It was too dark in the forest to see very far back and I sure didn't go back hunting for him."

Vern bent over, watched Amos's chest flutter with faint breathing, peered at the unconscious man's face, then straightened up and walked over to the stove.

"He's got something on his mind. He's got some kind of a plan. I'm as sure of that as I am of my own name, and I'd give a hundred dollars to know what he's up to."

The coffee began to boil. Vern got himself a bowl of cold and greasy venison stew, took it over to the table, and wearily sank down with his back to Mick and Ev. "Eat up," he ordered. "We're going after him all together as soon as I've finished here, and this time come hell or high water we won't quit until we get him."

Mick got the coffee pot, the three tin cups, and took them to the table. When Ev ladled two more bowls of that stew and brought them along, Mick shook his head. He couldn't eat those chunks of tough, dark meat lodged solidly in grease two inches thick if his life depended upon it.

Ev could, though, and he did. Hot coffee cut the grease for him. Ev was a man who'd missed enough meals in his lifetime to inspire him to gorge any time, any place he could.

"I don't like leaving the old man," Vern muttered. "But we got to, this time."

"He'll just lie there," opined Mick. "He doesn't

look as good this morning as he looked last night when he came out of it for a minute or two. I figure he won't move again until that sawbones gets up here."

"If then," said Ev, and got a bitter look from Vern. "Well, I mean it'll take a medical man to relieve the pressure or whatever's wrong with him, and he likely won't move until that's done."

Vern finished gulping his stew and cradled his tin cup in both hands, staring ahead at the bunkhouse door. He looked worn out from sleeplessness, worry, and tension. He also looked vicious.

"Where'll he be this time?" he asked softly, concentrating upon the yonder door.

"I'd guess either at Salt Valley or around here waiting to nail us when we step out this morning," suggested Ev.

"Or," put in Mick, "down at the hang tree again. We flushed him away from that spot and he'll maybe want to look around down there some more."

Vern sipped with both elbows on the table, holding his cup two handed. "I think so," he murmured. "One of those three places. But . . . which one?"

"We can eliminate the second one easily enough," stated Ev. "The minute we walk out of here, we'll either be shot at or not. If not . . . why then he ain't at the ranch."

But Vern shook his head about this. He kept staring over at the door, concentrating hard. "I don't think so, Ev. I'll tell you why . . . he could've potted me last night and he didn't."

Mick argued with this logic. "He didn't want just you. He wants all of us, Vern."

"Then tell me this, Mick . . . why didn't he start with me last night when I had my back to him?" Vern put down his cup, shook his head in disagreement, and arose from the table. "I thought about that on the way back. Thought about all of it. That's why I said earlier I'd give a hundred dollars to know what's in his mind. He's up to something, I tell you."

The other two also stood up away from the table. Mick went after his riding coat. Ev took their dishes and cups to the wash bucket and carelessly dumped them in, and afterward went after his coat.

Vern went over by old Amos's bunk, softly spoke his employer's name twice, got back not even a flicker of an eyelash, and sighed.

"He's bad off," he said softly. "Real bad off."

Neither Mick nor Ev commented on this. They'd just spent a gloomy night watching old Amos; they knew as well as Vern did that Amos McCarthy would never be the same man again whether he survived or not.

It was close to 5:00 now. There was that customary pre-daylight steely murk outside. It hung over everything except those northward mountains. There, sooty night still lingered, its gloominess augmented by the dark hide of trees, by the sharply cut high peaks, and by the eternally dark forest floor.

Ev methodically checked his shell belt and dumped more carbine cartridges into a coat pocket. This reminded Mick that he also needed more shells. Vern stood over by the door, watching those two until they were finished. He then lifted the latch, motioned toward the lamp, and stood still until Mick blew down the chimney, putting out the light.

Now the bunkhouse's interior glowed with that same uncertain gray that lay outside. As Mick started forward and angled past old Amos's bunk, he looked down. Amos hadn't moved in hours; it was impossible now to determine whether or not he was still breathing. He acted dead and he looked dead. Mick strode past and halted up beside Vern, awaiting Ev.

When they were all together, Vern eased the door back, sucked in an audible breath, and stepped forth. No gunshot erupted. Mick was next. Ev was last. Still there was no gunfire.

Ev, farthest back, heard Vern mutter a quick, soft—"Damn."—and craned around Mick to see what had brought this on. Vern's next words clarified it for Ev.

"My horse's gone."

Mick pushed on around the range boss, scanned the ring where Vern's saddle animal had been tied, turned slowly to scan the murky yard, saw no loose horse, and without a word stepped down, turned, and went hiking toward the barn.

The other two followed him, saying nothing. In each of their minds was the same hope and the same doubt. It was not at all unusual for tied horses to work themselves free to go ambling off. Under the circumstances, though, not even Mick, who initiated the search, felt in his secret heart that this is what had happened.

It was dark as midnight in the barn where they came together, still wordless, still searching with their narrowed eyes. Mick broke this pause by pushing on to the barn's rear, doorless opening, but this time when he halted, he was standing flat-footed with his shoulders slumped and his stony regard fixed dead ahead on the pole corrals where the other horses had been.

There was not a horse in sight.

Vern swore again as softly as before, but more fiercely this time.

Ev ventured farther out. He kept swinging his head as he approached the nearest gate as though he expected a gunshot, but the night ran on as hushed and breathlessly still as before.

"Plumb open," he quietly called back to Vern and Mick. "Open and braced back."

"Tell me the wind did that," Vern snarled to no one in particular. "Blew the latch open, then braced it open with a twig."

Ev came back to halt near Mick and look at his pardner. "Set us afoot, Mick," he said. "No one's going to ride off now."

"Now?" said Vern, looking quickly at Ev.

But Ev and Mick had exchanged their solemn and knowing look about that statement and Ev ignored the range boss.

"Good thing you went over to Beaver when you did," Mick told Vern, pulling him away from his other thought.

"Yeah," snarled the range boss. "Real good. Now we're afoot and that damned killer's lying out there somewhere, waiting."

"That can't be helped," retorted Mick irritably, annoyed by Vern's show of temper at a time when they needed clear heads. "We've got to go hunt up at least three of those horses, and we better get to doing it right now, too."

As Mick turned and swung back into the barn, heading for the lariat on his saddle, Vern and Ev started to turn, also. They were three feet apart and moving when, out of the pre-dawn paleness down by the creek, a bull-bass voice called over to them.

"You're afoot, boys! You got no chance at all now. Put aside your guns and let's talk. I want to . . ."

Vern's moving body was a blur. He whipped around, drew, and drowned out that recognizable voice with two blasting shots.

Ev, too, sprang clear of the rear opening and went for his gun. He fired from the hip with no target in sight, aiming in a general way toward that rumbling voice.

Farther up in the barn Mick yanked free his booted Winchester, dropped to one knee, and fired, too. He did not stop firing until he could see that both Vern and Ev were clear of the rear doorway.

Vern's back was to Mick and it was too black inside the old barn to make out anything more than movement, but Mick thought he saw the range boss suddenly jump up. He thought, too, that he understood what Vern was going to do.

"Don't!" he yelled. "Ev, stop him!"

Ev never got the chance. He'd only whipped his head around at Mick's frantic cry when Vern sprang over into the doorway with a wild bellow, jumped out, and dashed sideways for the protection of those southerly pole corrals.

Mick darted down where Ev was still crouching, his mouth hanging open, his eyes bulging in disbelief, and got down beside his pardner there to peer out.

Vern's low-held gun split the night with crimson lashes of flame as he went forward toward the creek in a zigzagging rush. He seemed bent on preventing Jackson from getting off any return shots.

"Too fast," said Mick shortly. "He's firing too fast. He'll fire himself empty. That's all Jackson's got to wait for."

Until now no gunfire had come from among the creek willows. Now it did, and at once Ev threw up his gun to fire directly at those onward tongues of flame. Mick, too, activated by Jackson's return fire, swung up his Winchester.

Jackson suddenly stopped firing. Mick surmised that, with lead slashing all around him, the unseen fugitive had been forced to break off and get away. He was right up to a point. Jackson moved all right, but only a hundred feet northward where the willows were even thicker, then he let go with one more gunshot. That one, Mick knew from experience, had been a steadily aimed, carefully aligned shot.

Ev bumped Mick's shoulder. "Vern's hit," he gasped. "Look yonder where the willows come up near the corrals."

Mick looked. He had missed seeing Vern initially rock backward until his shoulders struck corral stringers, but he saw him begin to slide down loosely, still with his back to those stringers, saw him settle lumpishly against the earth in a sitting posture with both hands hanging empty at his sides.

Mick crouched far over, rested his Winchester,

and fired into those northward willows where that solitary gunshot had come from. So did Ev. They kept it up until no more shots came back, then they ceased firing and a deep hush settled over Rafter M's yard.

Chapter Seventeen

In some ways the ensuing silence after all that gunfire was harder to bear than the explosions had been. Mick kept watching the humped-over silhouette where Vern Howten had gone down. He wanted to rush over there but prudence held him back. It wouldn't help any of them, Vern included, if Mick ran out and got shot, too.

Ev squirmed forward until he could see northward around the barn's rear opening. He was motionless for a long time.

In the first rank of trees northward someone spun out a horse and rode off, those sounds growing steadily smaller as the rider pushed on westerly.

Mick put aside his Winchester, drew his six-gun, and walked boldly out of the barn, heading in a straight line for Vern. Ev, remaining behind in firing position, kept his gun up, cocked and ready, even though he was satisfied that the rider they'd heard leaving was Holt Jackson.

Mick got up to Howten, kneeled, and pushed

his head down close. It was less difficult to see out where he now was than it had been in the barn, but it still wasn't light enough to make out where Jackson's slug had struck.

By the time Ev came up, Mick had the range boss stretched out, had his riding coat stripped off, and his wound adequately exposed.

"Plumb through the lungs, Ev. He's out like a light. Put up your gun and give me a hand getting him back to the bunkhouse."

Ev slowly holstered his weapon but he made no immediate move to grasp the unconscious range boss. "Jackson can shoot," he said. "Five inches to the left and he'd have drilled old Vern plumb through the heart. I call that fair shooting in the dark."

"Call it anything you want, just give me a hand here."

"Is he unconscious?"

"Yeah. Now quit talking and lend a hand."

They lifted Howten like a sack of meal between them, one holding his arms, one holding his legs. In this fashion they took him on around the barn, over to the bunkhouse, and inside. They dumped Vern on his own bunk and Mick crossed over to relight the lamp.

"We didn't get very far this morning," he said, lifting the chimney, applying a match to the ragged wick, and replacing the mantle. "Ev, he did a darned foolish thing, rushing out like that."

"Yeah. I didn't know he was doing it until I heard him beller and you yell. He's been on edge like that, though, since we found Amos."

Mick strolled over, saw how Ev had bared Howten's upper body, and dolorously wagged his head. "Bad," he pronounced. "Right through the lights. He'll bleed internally from that."

"The slug went through clean, though."

Mick went to the stove and poked up their coffee fire, filled a pan with water, and put it on to boil. He crossed over to look at Amos, lingered there a moment, then returned to Vern's bedside where Ev was wiping away blood with a rag.

"Must've really knocked him into those stringers for him to be unconscious this long. I knew a feller once who'd been lung-shot like that. He told me there wasn't any sensation of pain at all, just a sort of breathless feeling."

Ev twisted to squint upward. "How come," he asked gravely, "that every time we get into it with Jackson, one of us always gets hurt and him, never?"

"Amos hurt him. Remember that bleeding?"

Ev shook his head. "Then how come he's always waiting like he don't need any sleep? I tell you, Mick, that Jackson just ain't human."

"He's human all right. When we shredded those creek willows, he sure as hell got out of there."

Mick was turning to fetch the water when Vern groaned, opened his eyes, and lethargically

171

blinked as though through this effort he could bring his eyes to focus upon Ev, sitting on the edge of his bunk.

Mick and Ev were motionless, watching. After a long interval Vern groaned again, ran a tongue over his lips, and moved as though to lever himself up with his elbows.

Ev put forth a hand, holding the range boss down. "Steady," he admonished. "You're hurt, Vern. You stopped one through the lights."

Vern's eyes widened. He formed the word— "Shot?"—with his mouth and got an incredulous expression on his face.

Mick nodded down at him. "Shot," he confirmed. "Jackson got you square, down by the creek. Through the lungs, Vern. You better lie still for a while."

Vern's look of incredulity did not atrophy at once. He rolled both brows together in a concentrating effort to see those two close-by faces. He went limp under Ev's pushing hand and said huskily: "Deep six?"

Ev gently lifted his shoulders and let them fall, indicating by this that he did not know whether the wound was fatal or not. Vern looked from Ev to Mick, his stare inquiring.

Mick also shrugged. "I don't know, either," stated Mick quietly. "The doctor'll be along in a day or two. He'll know."

Vern's trauma was passing now. He formed

more words with his lips but this time he spoke them in an almost normal tone. "Did we get him?"

Mick, seeing the desperate hope in Howten's eyes, turned to get the water from the stove, leaving Ev to give Howten the disappointing answer to that.

"He run off," murmured Ev. "He had his horse back in the trees and he run off. Don't worry about it, though, we'll get him yet."

Vern's expression turned bitter. "Naw," he mumbled, his voice thickening. "Naw we won't." He rolled his head away from Ev.

Mick brought the hot water. Between them they thoroughly cleansed Howten's chest wound and tore up clean rags to make a cumbersome but effective bandage. By the time they were finished, the yonder ranch yard was filled with morning sunshine and increasing warmth.

Ev was washing his hands in the pink water when Mick brought him a cup of java. Ev looked at the stuff and wagged his head back and forth. "Can't do it," he said. "I swear my blood's plumb turned black from sopping up so much danged coffee these past few days."

Mick, sipping from his own cup, considered Ev for a moment before dryly saying: "We're in real trouble. I can tell for sure now, Ev. When you can't eat or drink, why then I know we're in bad trouble."

"And," muttered Ev, "I don't feel like joshing, either."

Mick crossed to the front window, peered out, and finished his coffee. Vern had been entirely correct; Jackson had been up to something. He'd set them afoot in a land where there was no hope of reaching aid without horses. Not only that, but Jackson had just about finished off Rafter M. From five confident men he'd whittled them down one at a time until only two remained.

"Mick?"

"Yeah."

"What do we do now?"

"Wait," said Mick from over at the window. "Just wait. We're boxed in here like a brace of cub bears. He's out there with broad daylight to help him. We're in here with two dying men . . . and not a horse in the corrals."

"You hungry, Mick?"

"Not hungry . . . worried and curious."

"Curious about what?"

Mick finally turned to face back into the room. Ev was seated over at the table looking ten years older than he had ten days earlier, older, bone-weary, and just about drained dry of spirit and resolve.

"Curious about why he always yells out before he opens up."

"He's got his reasons. Seven of 'em, and one of 'em his girl. Last night Vern said he couldn't figure out exactly why he didn't knife him when he had the chance. I reckon I know why that was. He wants the hide of every one of us, sure, but he wants more than just that. He aims to make each of us die a long time while we're still alive, before he pumps in the final bullet."

Mick considered this while swishing his coffee and watching its dark and oily swirls in the cup. "A lot of this I can't exactly figure out," he murmured, then crossed over and also sank down at the table. "I got a feeling something's bad wrong here, Ev."

"What particularly?"

"I don't know. I can't put my finger on it. It's just a sort of feeling I've got."

Mick put down the tin cup, pushed it away, and looked straight at his pardner. "He knows we're in here if he's still around. He knows Vern's hit. Then why doesn't he jeer a little out there from where we can't see him to get a shot? Why isn't he ragging us about whittling away until only you and me are left?"

"I don't know," muttered Ev tiredly. "Right this minute I don't really care a whole lot. I'm about wore down to a nubbin from going day and night without sleep."

Ev pushed upright, turned, went over, and looked down at Vern. "How do you feel?" he quietly asked.

Howten neither looked up at Ev nor answered,

although both his eyes were wide open and fixed dryly upon the slats of the bunk above where he lay.

Ev walked on to his own bunk and eased down upon the edge of it. He looked at Mick over at the table. He also gazed upon the still, ashen face of old Amos on across the room. He removed his hat, his coat, dumped both upon the floor, ran a hand through his hair, and leaned far back, placing both shoulders against the rough log wall across his bunk. For a long time he sat like that, saying nothing and not especially looking at anything.

Mick, too, seemed unusually quiet for a while, but he lacked the morose, dejected expression of Ev, and eventually he stood up saying: "I'd rather be shot at than stay in here. Between your face and these two wounded fellers . . ." He didn't finish it, but strolled to the door, let his hand rest uncertainly upon the latch, and whether he meant to leave the bunkhouse or not, was distracted in either event when Vern Howten wetly said: "He ain't out there."

Mick turned. Vern was looking steadily over at him. The range boss' eyes seemed drowsy, his voice was a little slurred.

"He ain't out there, Mick. He's up to something else now. If he was out there, he'd let you know it by now."

Vern's voice trailed off. Mick stood a while, watching Howten; he was turning those statements over in his mind slowly and skeptically, that much was obvious from his expression. He slowly lifted the latch, eased the door open, and waited briefly, then stepped through where sunlight dazzlingly struck him at once.

Ev, brought out of his depthless dejection by this, slowly pushed forward to the edge of his bunk, slowly got up, and went over to the door.

Mick was standing out there, wide-legged, his right hand hooked, his right elbow bent to draw, his nostrils extended.

No shot came, no one called out, no movement anywhere indicated that Holt Jackson was around. Mick slowly straightened up and relaxed his muscles. Without facing around, he said: "Vern was right. He isn't out here."

"Why not?"

Mick shook his head. "I don't know. I can't for the life of me figure this Jackson feller out, unless . . . unless it's like you said a while back. Unless he wants to stretch this thing out until we're worn down to frazzles by the damned waiting."

Ev stepped forth onto the bunkhouse's little porch and at once had to pucker his eyelids against that dazzling sunlit brightness. He closed the door behind and said: "If we got a chance, Mick, we'd better use it finding our cussed horses. You game?"

Mick stepped down into the yard. "Let's go,"

he said, and struck out boldly, in plain sight, for the barn where his lariat still hung upon the swells of his saddle. Ev moved out, too, and although Ev was just as bold, he kept his head swinging from side to side until, inside the barn, his doubts vanished as his puzzlement increased.

Chapter Eighteen

As they hiked up into the trees, each with his lariat, crossed the intervening open distance between Rafter M's buildings and the forest, Mick said: "It doesn't make sense, Ev. Why isn't he around to pot us?"

"Gave up, maybe," responded Ev, but with no conviction of this in his voice. "Gave up and rode on out, or gone somewhere to catch up on his sleep."

Mick halted in deep shadows and shook his head, gazing back down at the ranch buildings. "I don't believe that," he muttered.

"Then maybe we hit him hard in the fight at the barn."

Mick considered this, found it much more plausible, and said so. He then turned eastward and led out through the trees. There were no horse tracks to guide him, but he felt reasonably sure their loose horses would have gone in this direction because it led down and around behind the granite rimrocks and on out to the southerly grasslands.

The morning was well along now. Benign warmth loosened weary muscles, brought on a relentless drowsiness, made Mick slow his brisk steps a mile farther onward, and finally inclined Ev to say: "Let's rest a minute. I'm plumb drug out."

They sat together at the base of a red-barked old shaggy fir tree, made a smoke, and looked at the southward range, just now becoming visible, but only partly so, as the land forms southward broke up a little, began to sink down low before rising again toward the more easterly rims. There was a haze southward but neither man thought anything of it. Running horses could make that, or dusting cattle.

"Mick, after we get the horses, how're we going to get him? The son-of-a-gun's got an uncanny way of anticipating everything we try."

"We won't go after him next time, Ev. We'll do what we should've done right from the start. We'll go back to the ranch and wait. Let him come to us this time."

Ev took a long last drag off his smoke, punched the thing hard down into the ground killing it, and nodded. "Yeah," he assented. "I reckon you're right. We wait him out in the bunkhouse or the barn . . . some place where we got cover and he's got to cross open ground to get at us."

Ev stood up, looking fresher. He cocked his head for a look at the overhead morning sun, lowered it, and said when this was over, he was going to sleep for a week. He stepped out with Mick and within a very short time they were making the initial climb to the rims. It was in both their minds that if their horses were down on the prairie, they'd be able to see them from up there.

Mick made the top-out first. When he straightened up, pushed clear of the screening juniper limbs, and stepped forth upon the wind-polished stone of that eminence, he halted dead still, and for a second stopped breathing.

Far ahead, making that dust they'd seen earlier, were two wagons, each with riders around them.

Ev came up, breathing hard, saw those distant vehicles boring along through bright sunlight, and gasped. For as long as it took for both of them to piece together several connecting factors neither of them spoke.

Mick lifted his right arm, pointed rigidly westerly, and said: "There are the tracks, fresh in the dew and grass, Ev. Those wagons and riders came from that direction."

"Who are they? What're they doing down there?"

Mick dropped his arm, swung his head, and studied the oncoming wagons for a long time in total silence. "Wish we'd brought old Amos's binoculars," he said very quietly. "I think maybe they've been to the hang tree, Ev."

"Good Lord," whispered Everett. "They'll be cronies of Jackson's. Mick, there's at least twelve of 'em. We're sunk for sure now."

Mick remained stiff with concentration as he watched those approaching wagons with their escorting armed riders. "Now I know why he set us afoot. So we couldn't any of us leave the country before he had all his answers. But I'd sure like to know why he didn't use his friends in his fight with us Rafter M fellers."

Ev made no comment, no speculation on this latest mystery. He simply stood up there beside Mick, watching balefully from red-rimmed eyes that slow-grinding cavalcade down there that was coming ahead with agonizing slowness.

They were both wholly absorbed in looking southward and were entirely unaware that they were not alone upon the rim until a man's rough voice spoke gently to them from out of sight rearward, and very close by, so close in fact that it instantly struck them both that, standing out there completely exposed as they were, with no cover anywhere around, their alternative to remaining absolutely still was death.

"Boys, put your hands high up and don't make a false move."

Mick's breath ran out in a soft sigh. He raised both arms. At his side Ev stiffened, seemed to brace himself for the shot in the back he expected, and also raised his arms.

For what seemed an eternity there were no more words, no sounds of any kind behind them. It did not appear to either of them that their captor could make up his mind what he should do next. But this proved to be an incorrect surmise, for both their holstered six-guns lifted clear even though they had heard no movement to indicate their captor had got up behind them.

"Now turn around," ordered that same rough but gentle voice.

Mick turned first. Ev was a little slower. Mick found himself looking straight into the drawn, gray face of the man he'd met at Salt Valley the day he'd pulled that hung-up calf—Holt Jackson.

For a full minute the three of them exchanged an unblinking stare. Jackson stepped back, eased off the hammer of his gun, pushed it into a hip holster, and tossed aside the pair of weapons he'd taken from Mick and Ev. He did all this without looking away or saying a word. He next reached into a shirt pocket, withdrew something, held forth his left hand, and opened it. There was a U.S. marshal's badge lying in his palm.

Ev's mouth sagged. Mick gradually lowered both his arms until they hung at his sides. He was dumbfounded, too, but more than that, he was beginning to feel a little sick at the stomach.

"You two are under arrest," said Jackson, using that same quiet tone of voice. "You know why, don't you?"

Mick looked up. "Tell us," he said.

"Murder. Resisting arrest. Assaulting an officer of the law in performance of his duty. Concealing a felony. That enough, Mick?"

Mick shifted his feet, hooked both thumbs in his shell belt, and seemed to come out of the utter amazement that had held him a moment before. Ev, though, was still staring, bug-eyed, over at Holt Jackson. He still had both arms rigidly over his head.

"Mister," stated Mick. "We didn't know you were a law officer. Didn't any of us knowingly resist arrest."

"Who'd you think I was, Mick?"

Now Ev spoke. He said: "One of . . . them."

Jackson's sunken eyes swerved to consider Ev briefly, then swung back to Mick. There was irony in their depths. "One of them?" he said, raising the inflexion of that last word, making a question of it.

Mick said flatly. "You know damned well who he's talking about. Tell me something, Mister Jackson, who are those men down there with the wagons? What've they been doing this morning?"

Jackson reached up, thumbed back his broad-brimmed black Stetson, and said: "To answer that I've got to back a little ways, Mick. To start with, I saw one of you leave the ranch last night a-horseback."

"That'd be Vern," muttered Ev, bringing his arms down finally.

"All right, Vern then. I didn't know who he was but I figured he was making that ride for a purpose, so I trailed him. You boys know where he led me? Over to a big cow outfit west of here owned by a man named Charley Beaver. Until he led me over there, I didn't know there was another ranch anywhere around. But then, like I told you, Mick, I was new in the country."

"Why didn't you kill Vern, mister?" Ev asked.

Jackson looked surprised. "Kill him? Hell, I just wanted to know where he was going. I didn't want to kill any of you. I tried to tell you that . . . tried to tell you who I was every time we met. But you boys never gave me a chance. You opened up like I was the whole Sioux nation on the warpath every time I tried to tell you I was the law.

"Anyway, to get back to your friend . . . after he'd been at the Beaver place and started back, I went on in, introduced myself, deputized the men over there, and sent 'em down to your hang tree with their wagons this morning."

"I see," murmured Mick. "You didn't trail Vern back to Rafter M, after all."

"No. I didn't leave the Beaver Ranch until way late. Then I slipped into Rafter M, set your saddle stock loose so couldn't any of you leave the country . . . and waited until you two came out this morning horse hunting. I followed you here and you know the rest."

Jackson plunged a hand into a trousers pocket, brought it out, and dangled a little locket from his fingers in the dazzling sunlight.

Mick looked, nodded, and said: "Yeah, we've seen it before. You took it off old Amos."

"That's right. That cussed old he-wolf tried to stalk me. I knew one of you would try it sooner or later."

"You crushed his skull, Jackson."

"I know. But not with the first blow I didn't. That old devil was tough with a skull like iron. He knifed me in the arm before I could hit him harder, the second time."

Ev said dully: "Mister, this is just now beginning to make sense to me. You're not her husband at all, are you?"

Jackson palmed the little gold locket. He looked at it a long time and shook his head. "No, I'm not her husband, and it didn't occur to me right away why you Rafter M fellows were trying so hard to salt me down." He raised his eyes to Ev's face. "I've been thinking about that. I reckon you figured you had to kill me, too, or I'd kill you, is that it?"

Both Mick and Ev nodded. Mick said: "It was those initials in that locket."

The U.S. marshal pocketed the little locket. "Coincidence," he said. "That saddle I left on your bunkhouse porch . . . that was her husband's outfit. His name was Howard Jerrold. Same initials but not much similarity in our names."

"Ahh," breathed Ev. "Mick, he was the other one . . . the feller Vern shot in the leg, the feller who went crazy when he saw her hanging up there."

Mick said nothing for a while. Southward and below the rimrocks those creaking wagons made their sad, sad sounds.

"I don't feel good," Mick finally said, and sat down. "Lord, Ev, the whole thing went wrong right from the start."

Holt Jackson also eased down upon the wind-swept, smooth stone. He looked from one of them to the other. He said in an altered tone of voice: "Boys, the old days and the old ways are no more. I don't reckon the law'll do a whole lot to either of you for this. Maybe, if one of 'em hadn't been a girl, it wouldn't do anything at all. Rustlers are outlaws and folks got a right to protect themselves from 'em. But from now on . . . not like you fellows did. Those days are done for. You got caught between two systems . . . the old and the new."

"Marshal, we had no idea *that* one was a girl until we went back to bury 'em. She was dressed just like the others." Mick looked squarely at

Marshal Holt Jackson. "About the rest of it . . . if you'd showed me that badge the day we met up in Salt Valley, maybe the rest of this wouldn't have happened."

Jackson inclined his head. "I couldn't show you the badge then. I didn't know you. I didn't know what I was up against in these uplands. But even if I had, Mick, I don't think that old devil who tried to knife me would have acted any different."

Mick thought on this briefly. He concluded bitterly that Jackson was probably right on that point. Old Amos wouldn't have been stopped by that badge.

The wagons swung westerly now at the base of the rimrocks and their creaking, their groaning was louder.

Mick said: "You had those deputized men from Beaver dig 'em up, Mister Jackson?"

"Yeah. It wasn't hard to figure out what'd happened or where you buried 'em." Jackson got up, peered down at those wagons, said: "Come on. They're heading for Rafter M. Let's get back there and wait for 'em, boys." He paused, watching Mick come upright. "I'd like your word it's all over."

Mick nodded. So did Ev. They shuffled on around the U.S. marshal with the ghastly, tragic sound of those moving wagons down below. Jackson moved in behind them. The three of them started back for McCarthy's ranch, unaware that within Rafter M's bunkhouse two men lay dead and sightlessly staring at the blackened ceiling of the bunkhouse of an old-time cow ranch.

Jackson made one more comment just before they got back to Rafter M. He said: "I've been trailing that rustler band for three months, but never, in my wildest dreams, did I think it might end like this."

About the Author

Lauran Paine who, under his own name and various pseudonyms has written over a thousand books, was born in Duluth, Minnesota. His family moved to California when he was at a young age and his apprenticeship as a Western writer came about through the years he spent in the livestock trade, rodeos, and even motion pictures where he served as an extra because of his expert horsemanship in several films starring movie cowboy Johnny Mack Brown. In the late 1930s, Paine trapped wild horses in northern Arizona and even, for a time, worked as a professional farrier. Paine came to know the Old West through the eyes of many who had been born in the 19th Century, and he learned that Western life had been very different from the way it was portrayed on the screen. "I knew men who had killed other men," he later recalled. "But they were the exceptions. Prior to and during the Depression, people were just too busy eking out an existence to indulge in Saturday-night brawls." He served in the U.S. Navy in the Second World War and began writing for Western pulp magazines following his discharge. It is interesting to note that all of his earliest novels (written under his own name and the pseudonym

Mark Carrel) were published in the British market and he soon had as strong a following in that country as in the United States. Paine's Western fiction is characterized by strong plots, authenticity, an apparently effortless ability to construct situation and character, and a preference for building his stories upon a solid foundation of historical fact. ADOBE EMPIRE (1956), one of his best novels, is a fictionalized account of the last twenty years in the life of trader William Bent and, in an off-trail way, has a melancholy, bittersweet texture that is not easily forgotten. In later novels like THE WHITE BIRD (1997) and CACHE CAÑON (1998), he showed that the special magic and power of his stories and characters had only matured along with his basic themes of changing times, changing attitudes, learning from experience, respecting Nature, and the yearning for a simpler, more moderate way of life.

Center Point Large Print
600 Brooks Road / PO Box 1
Thorndike, ME 04986-0001 USA

(207) 568-3717

US & Canada:
1 800 929-9108
www.centerpointlargeprint.com